I0846905

Never Say Never

Judy Giddens Sheriff, Ph.D.

Never Say Never

Finding Love After Loss

Never Say Never: Finding Love After Loss

ISBN: 979-8-218-26650-9
Library of Congress Control Number: 2023918141
Edited by Elizabeth Boerner
Typeset and cover design by Helen Ounjian
Cover photo: "Spring Daisies" by Eerik, Getty Images for Canva

Printed in the United States of America

Perfect Misfits LLC
An Independent Publishing Company
For inquiries, email perfectmisfits.de@gmail.com

This book is dedicated to my husband, Richard, who honorably and faithfully served our country in the USMC, with 14 months in Viet Nam. He was wounded in combat and was the recipient of two Purple Heart medals. He is the love of my life.

A huge heart-felt thank you goes to all who have served our country through our five military branches. The sacrifices you made are not forgotten and are forever engraved in our hearts.

To all who have been left behind after suffering the loss of your loved one in battle, let me assure you that through your pain, suffering, and loss, God can and will bring healing to your broken hearts. The emptiness you feel can sometimes blind you from seeing how God can heal and bring wholeness to your life again. Open your heart to the healing process and be willing to open your heart to love again. God is good. He is faithful. He will be with you.

Remember – *Never Say Never!*

One

Her small delicate fingers lightly traced the outline of the triangular shaped shadow box which held an American flag neatly and militarily folded. On the bottom of the frame was a small gold plaque which read, *Colonel Tyler D. Barrett, USMC.* She still felt the impact of that day when the young Marine placed it in her hands and softly whispered, *"On behalf of a grateful nation, the United States Marine Corps, and the President of the United States, please accept this flag as a symbol of our appreciation for your loved one's honorable and faithful service."* It all happened five years ago, yet it seemed like only yesterday.

It was just an ordinary day in the life of Ellie Barrett. Her day began the same as every day – a shower, coffee, her usual yogurt and blueberries, and a strong hope that she would get a phone call from Tyler. Although he was serving in Iraq, he managed to call as often as he could. Ellie had not seen Tyler in almost a year and his phone calls were a solace to her aching heart, longing to feel his arms around her again. He meant everything to her. Their life together was one that so many people only dream of. Best friends, lovers, parents, and they shared every thought, every fear, every joy and every hope for their future. They were as tightly woven as the strongest strands of the largest hemp rope.

She gazed again at the flag in the shadow box and it all tumbled back to her mind as she recalled that life-changing day and how it all happened. As she stood in her kitchen, hoping for the phone call from Tyler, she heard the chiming of her door bell. Broken from her thoughts of him, she quickly walked to the door. Opening it, she saw the very image she feared the most. In military attire, standing tall and erect, two high-ranking officers looked at her. She knew!

"Mrs. Ellie Barrett?" Ellie knew what was coming next. "May we come in?"

She stepped aside, heart pounding in her chest, and beads of perspiration forming on her body and an overwhelming weakness in her knees. In her mind, she prayed, *Please, God, not Tyler. Please, God, not now.* She led the men into her den, sat in her husband's favorite recliner, and waited for the news. It all seemed so surreal. She wasn't fully aware of how her trembling hands were massaging the leather chair as she listened. This just couldn't be happening, not to Tyler. He was always so careful and so aware of his surroundings in Iraq. What she was hearing from these men seemed so far away in her mind – like a whisper in the wind. When she faintly heard them say Tyler's body would be arriving in 3 days, she completely lost her composure. Sobbing, she managed to thank them and quickly showed them to the door as they continued to offer their condolences. Even in the midst of tremendous sorrow and shock, she knew their task had to rate at the top of their list of the most difficult and heartbreaking tasks they would ever have to do – and she knew this wasn't their first or their last time for doing this. Somehow in the shock and horror of all of it, she also felt saddened for these men who always had the strenuous task of having to tell families of their loss. As she heard their car drive away, she leaned against the door and slid to the floor, completely engulfed in her tears.

She sobbed and cried out, "Oh, God, what am I going to do without Tyler? How can I tell the children?" Their daughter, Annie, was in a nearby town and could come home immediately. Their son, Mark, was almost an hour from home, which she was certain that he would make the trip in record time. Annie would be there to help Ellie as they waited for Mark. There were so many things to take care of, so many people to call, and arrangements to be made. The list went on and on swimming, swirling inside Ellie's head. Still crying uncontrollably, she knew she had to make the call to her children. They would be devastated. Their Dad was the rock of the family, the one they all went to for advice and encouragement. How was she going to tell them that their father was coming home – but this time he would be in a flag-draped casket!

That dreaded day arrived, and Ellie and the children were at the airport to receive their beloved husband and father. They watched as the soldiers reverently slid the casket from the rear door of the plane and marched with their hands tightly gripped on the brass handles. How could this be happening? This was never supposed to be the way she would greet her husband from Iraq. Ellie's heart felt as if it would explode in her chest into a million pieces as the soldiers and Tyler's body quietly and quickly slipped away. She knew the plans for the funeral had been made and now she had to wait for the day of the service – only three days away.

So many people! So many sad and mourning eyes watching her! The service was a typical military service and one she would cherish in her heart forever. Words of kindness, admiration, condolence all were directed towards her and her family. The flag, the salutes, the music – everything that could possibly make her heart ache even more, did, but she wanted to honor Tyler and his service to our country in every way possible. Ellie knew that following the service she would have to make her way to the National Cemetery for the burial. The ride seemed to take an eternity as they all stared at the tree-lined streets and the children playing in their yards. No one knew what was happening inside their car or the car that carried their loved one. Life was going on as usual, no worries or cares about Ellie and her children. As they arrived at the cemetery plot where the green tent was placed over Tyler's grave, she was sure that she couldn't bear it any longer. Her heart once again pounded in her chest and she could hear Annie and Mark whispering to each other, their words muffled by their sobs.

Approaching the tent, she saw the flag-covered casket hovering over the deep hole where it would be lowered. She cried quietly, but only moments before taking her seat on the front row, she cried uncontrollably. Someone from behind handed her a tissue. She knew one tissue couldn't possibly hold the tears that would flow from her already red and swollen eyes.

At the end of the graveside service the young Marines meticulously folded the flag and Ellie could hear each snap and fold. Her heart was breaking. One of the young Marines slowly walked to Ellie, knelt in front of her, and presented her with the flag. Her trembling hands gently took it and tears streamed down her face as she thanked him.

Ellie wasn't sure how she managed to get through that service at the cemetery, but it was only by God's grace that she did. It had to be her strong faith in God that kept her intact. She felt a calmness and a peace that only comes from God, even in the midst of the most difficult time of her life and even amid the tears. She and Tyler had talked about the possibility of something like this happening, but she never thought it would actually come to pass. They discussed their faith in God and of His assurance that He would see them through anything that happened in their lives. Today she had to exercise that faith, no matter how difficult it was. She gripped the flag that was presented to her and held it close to her heart as she and Annie and Mark walked to the car. The next few hours were going to be just as difficult.

Arriving at their home, the three of them slowly and hesitantly walked into the house. It was filled with people and noise – some laughter and some sniffles of sadness. Immediately, friends approached her and the children and began with their condolences. Mentally, Ellie prayed, *Dear God, I don't think I can take any more today. I know these people mean well, but my heart is broken, and I need some time alone. Please help me be gracious and in control of my broken-heartedness until they all leave.* God heard and He answered. She was able to personally greet each person, and even though she kept glimpsing at the folded flag on the table, she stood tall and in control. In her mind, she kept wishing everyone would hurry and leave. She kept thinking, *How much food can all these people eat? There is a huge buffet and they keep eating and eating and returning for more. Don't they know I need this time for myself and my children? Please hurry and allow me time to grieve.* Ellie immediately felt guilty for even having such thoughts about these lovely people who had come to pay their respects.

It was as if everyone heard her mental prayer at once, for soon everyone started hugging her and the children, and making their way to the door. In a matter of minutes everyone was gone except three ladies from their church who told Ellie to go to her room, change her clothes, lie down for awhile and they would see to all the cleaning up and putting away food in the kitchen. She didn't argue with them about any of it and quickly did as they asked. The last thing on her mind was cleaning up all the mess, the food, the plates, the crumbs. She just wanted to be alone. Her children had already skirted away to their own rooms, possibly beginning the grieving process in their own way.

It was in her room that she felt the real pain and loss. As she closed the door behind her, she slowly glanced around the room, looking at the bed she and Tyler had shared for so many years. Without changing her clothes, she limply fell down on Tyler's side of the bed and scrunched his pillow beneath her chin and close to her heaving chest. The tears started and fell like a never-ending waterfall. Ellie wasn't sure how long she had stayed in that position and cried, but she did know that the sun had set, the room was filled with the reflection of pinkish gray clouds. Glancing at the clock, she realized she had been in that one position for almost four hours. The pillow was soaked with her tears. This was Tyler's pillow, the one she had slept with for months, nestled close to her every night while he was in Iraq. And now, these tears that saturated the pillow were tears of pain, loneliness, fear, and deep-rooted anguish. How could she possibly face another day?

Ellie heard the whispers outside her bedroom door and robotically managed to pull herself from the bed and walk to the door. As she opened it, she saw Annie and Mark, standing there. Their eyes were red from crying. "Mom, are you alright? What can we do for you?"

Ellie should have been asking the same thing of her children, but when she heard the pain and loss in their shaky voices, she began to cry again and the three of them stood in a tight huddle, sharing tears and sobs, and tiny whispers of prayer.

They made their way to the neatly cleaned kitchen and thought they should eat something since none of them had eaten all day. Their stomachs suddenly felt too full to even try to eat. Their attempts were futile. Annie made a pot of coffee and the three of them sat down in front of a fire that Mark had already built. They sat in silence, sipping coffee, each one not knowing what to say.

The silence was broken by Ellie's quiet, raspy voice. The sweet soft voice that usually came from her was now hollow and rough from the crying and screaming into Tyler's pillow.

Leaning on her strength from God, Ellie straightened her shoulders and faced her children. "Okay, we have had an exhausting day – one filled with much loss and pain for all of us. Tonight we will all rest and pray that God will give us a new tomorrow with clear minds to take care of the things we need to do. I know we will each grieve in our own way and in our own time, as well as the length of time it will take, but we MUST grieve so we can begin to heal. Take all the time you need, do whatever you need to do to bring healing to your own lives. I will do the same. We must also remember that we are all here for each other and we will lean on each other whenever we need to. Do you both agree to this?" Too filled with tears to be able to speak, they only nodded and then went to their rooms. Ellie was surprised at how well she handled that, but she also knew that God had given her the words and the strength to convey it all to the children. *What a wonderful and loving God,* Ellie thought.

Ellie wasn't sure how Annie and Mark would get through the night, but she knew she needed to pray for them first and then she would deal with her own pain. On her knees beside her bed, she began to pour out her heart to God for her children. First, she thanked Him for blessing their home with two beautiful and healthy children who were living so close to God. Their lives were such a blessing to everyone they met. She and Tyler had prayed for years that their children would see their need for a Savior and would eventually give their lives to Him. At least Tyler was alive to see it all come to fruition. She prayed for their hurting and lonely hearts – that God would begin to fill that void for them. Her prayer was interspersed with tears. How could there possibly be so many tears!

She didn't know how long she had been praying for the children, but she was soon overcome with weariness and climbed into bed, fully clothed, and slept on Tyler's side of the bed, along with the wet pillow tucked close to her heart. Sleep finally overtook her body. All of this seemed so far in the past and yet, it seemed like only a few minutes ago when it all happened.

Ellie was a million miles away in thought while she continued to trail her fingers across the shadow box. She was holding it tightly to her chest when the door flew open and the usual sweet voice of Annie bounced through the air. "Mom, I'm home, and I am starving for one of your home-cooked meals, or we could…." She stopped mid-sentence as she stared at her mother holding the shadow box.

"Mom, are you alright? What are you doing and why are you holding Dad's flag? Is anything wrong? Please, Mom, talk to me."

Gently smiling and with a tiny ache in her heart, she replied, "Oh, Annie, it's okay. I was just having one of my moments. They come often, but not as often as they did in the beginning. I have sweet memories of your Dad, and today I guess I was just in a melancholy mood. Everything is fine." She placed the shadow box back on the mantel next to the gold-framed picture of her handsome and loving Tyler.

"Now, what did you say about wanting one of my home-cooked meals? I don't have too many of those anymore since you and Mark are away from home and beginning your new careers. Tell me what you'd like to have and I'll get busy in the kitchen. Or, if you'd rather, we can go out to dinner."

It was decided – Ellie would prepare Annie's favorite meal, deep-dish baked spaghetti smothered in mozzarella cheese served with a salad and garlic bread.

There was small talk during dinner and Annie filled her Mom in on all her activities, while also slipping into the conversation that there was a special young man that she was seeing. Ellie's ears perked up. "Well, honey, tell me about him. I want to know everything – I think!" They both laughed and it seemed so refreshing to Ellie to hear laughter in the house once again.

Later that evening, after Annie had received that special phone call from her new boyfriend, she and Ellie sat down to relax and talk, mother to daughter. In the background, the television was on and although neither of them was watching, they knew it was one of those "too-good-to-be-true" Hallmark movies.

Annie began the conversation. "Mom, I know you and Dad had the most wonderful marriage ever. Mark and I often commented on how we hoped one day that each of us could find that special someone and we could have a marriage just like yours and Dad's."

Ellie was waiting for what she knew was coming next. She wasn't ready to hear it, but she knew what Annie was going to say was the truth. In her mind, she didn't want to face it.

"Mom, you know Mark and I love you and we want you to be happy. It's been five years since Dad has been gone. Don't you think you need to start thinking about a new life for yourself?"

Ellie curled her legs beneath her, held tight to a small sofa pillow and lovingly said, "Annie, I know you mean well, and I understand why you're saying this. Yes, it's been five years, but Annie, to me it feels like only yesterday. Your Dad was everything to me and I just don't think I can even entertain the thoughts of dating again. I wouldn't even know how. Things are so different these days and men aren't always looking for an older woman. It seems they all want younger women with long legs, beautiful long blonde hair, and perky bosoms!" She couldn't help but laugh at what she had just said, and Annie giggled at her mother's description. "What in the world do I have to offer? No, Annie, thank you, but I'm perfectly happy with my life." It even sounded humorous to Ellie, but it also sounded as truth

"Happy with your life? Mom, you don't do anything!" She was almost shouting at Ellie. "You stay at home and probably watch all the Hallmark movies of how things are supposed to be. You work in your flower garden, go to church, visit the grocery store, and go home. What kind of life is that? You and Dad used to go bowling, go to ballgames, frequent the ice cream shop, and go on little weekend get-a-ways. Don't you miss doing those things? Don't you get tired of just staying home all the time?"

Ellie knew Annie was right, but she had no idea how to even begin again. Her whole life had been lovingly wrapped up in her devoted and loving husband and children and now they were all gone – Annie and Mark no longer at home, and her husband was now in Heaven. It was just all too difficult to imagine trying to begin a new life with a new man. Nope, this wasn't for Ellie. No one could take Tyler's place. Her heart had no room for another man – it just wouldn't seem right. *I will NEVER give my heart to another man.* That mental statement bounced around in her head. Never, never, never!

Two

"What an absolutely glorious day God has given." Ellie's praises were spoken aloud. She awoke with somewhat of a new spring in her step. She wasn't sure why she was feeling this way, but she liked it. It felt good! She felt good! The whole world felt good! What in the world was happening to her? She had not felt this way since she and Tyler spent the weekend on a nearby lake in a quaint cabin – just the two of them. She recalled how giddy she felt riding next to him that day, like a teenager on a first date – except she and Tyler had been married for many years. They knew each other completely and sometimes it felt as if they knew the very thoughts of the other one. Closely knit and deeply in love; that was Tyler and Ellie. Together, alone for a weekend in this cozy cabin. She remembered every detail of their time, every intimate moment they shared, and the laughter that echoed through the woods and across the lake as they playfully termed themselves as "recycled teenagers." What a blessing they were to each other.

Her pain and loss had healed significantly, although she thought of him every day and still missed him. There were times when she would cry with no apparent warning or reason. However, she knew the reason was that she was still missing her husband and even though it had been years since he passed away, he seemed to crawl slowly up from the depths of her heart and emerge in full force, leaving her breathless and usually in tears. Times like these were beginning to be less and less, but when they did hit, they hit hard and strong. She would have her crying spell, and then she'd feel better.

Reeling herself back to reality, she began to feel fresh and new and the words of her daughter kept coming to the forefront of her mind. *Mom, you need to start thinking about a new life for yourself.* She chuckled as she looked in the mirror; she spoke aloud to the reflection in the mirror. "Me, Ellie Barrett, start again – dating? Absolutely not! No way! Never in a million years! My life is great as it is. I love my flower garden. I love my time alone with a good book. My house cleaning is so therapeutic." As she went on and on with her flimsy list of hum-drum activities, she started to feel the pangs of loneliness. Maybe it was time for her to begin to think about her future. "Oh, this just isn't going to work," moaned Ellie. "Now, back to my mental list of things to do today."

With such a beautiful day, Ellie tried to mentally line up the things she wanted to do. Too many things swirled around in her mind, so she tore a page from her notebook she kept on her neat marble countertop and began to scribble her notes for the day. The first item on her list was to give her bedroom an extremely good cleaning – top to bottom. During the years, she had cleaned it, but it just seemed like today was the day to go into every nook and cranny and clean until everything was spotless. This first item would probably take most of her day. Not only did she need to clean the room, but she also needed to begin to clean the cobwebs from her life – although she didn't realize it at the moment, this would be exactly what she needed for today and for her future!

Searching, and successfully gathering the mop, bucket, vacuum, dust cloths and furniture polish, she made her way to her bedroom. Gazing at the walls, she thought perhaps it was time for a new color, new bedding and curtains, and maybe even new furniture. Those pangs of pain hit as she thought of giving up the very bed that she and Tyler had shared so many conversations and so many wonderful intimate moments as husband and wife. Ellie pushed the thought of new furniture to the back of her mind. Even after five years, it still hurt each time she got into her bed and reached for Tyler only to be tapped in her heart again at the empty spot.

After much scrubbing, cleaning, and re-arranging, she decided to open the walk-in closet to sort through clothes. There it was! Again, her mind raced back to the day she had to clean out the closet and make a decision about what she should do with Tyler's clothes. She leaned against the wall as she recalled that day.

She had waited over a year before she could even think about removing his clothes from their closet. She just couldn't do it. It would be like taking away his memory – the only thing she had left that she could cling to. Yet, she knew it was time. She remembered how she slowly fingered each shirt, even putting her nose to each one to see if she could still smell his cologne. Immediately after his death, she would cling to every piece of clothing trying to "feel" his arms in the sleeves of his shirts or touch the jeans and be reminded of his strong lithe body in them. She had touched his shoes and boots and could almost feel his perfectly formed feet in them. Inside one of his sports coats, she found a receipt from one of the fancier restaurants he had taken her to on her birthday. Stuffed in another coat pocket were a monogrammed handkerchief and a button that had popped off his shirt. He had never told her about the button. Such little things, but they were things that his hands had touched. She remembered how she held them in her hand and kept gingerly touching each item. As she continued to look in the closet filled with his clothes, she saw all the neckties he had kept through the years, even though some of them were completely out of date – but the children had given him a tie every Father's Day for years. He had saved them all. So many clothes and she wondered how and if she could remove them, leaving an empty space. It just seemed that it would be giving the message that he no longer resided there, that he was actually gone forever, and it was almost sacrilegious to give them away. Yet, she knew it was time. Carefully and lovingly, she had gathered up all the clothes that belonged to Tyler and put them in a neat pile on one of the chairs in the bedroom. She immediately called Annie and Mark to tell them what she was doing and invited them to come by at their convenience and go through the clothes to select anything they would like to have that belonged to their dad. There! She had done it! That was a big step for her. It was part of a therapeutic healing for Ellie Barrett.

Ellie pulled her thoughts to the present time. So today was cleaning and scrubbing day in her bedroom. The empty closet on Tyler's side was bare and had been for a few years. But in her peripheral vision something caught her attention. What was that on the shelf shoved in the back of the closet and how had she missed it so long ago? She jumped to try to reach it, but her short stature hindered her. Hurriedly, she ran to the utility room, picked up the small folding step stool and returned to the closet. Steadily, she climbed up and stretched her arm to the far corner of the shelf. "Oh, my goodness, what is this?" she spoke to herself. Stepping down from the stool, she took the small black velvet box and sat on the edge of her bed. All sorts of thoughts ran through her mind. *Why was it in the back corner? Who did it belong to? Was Tyler having an affair and this was a gift for his mistress and was he trying to hide it from her – never dreaming he would never make it home to give it to the mystery woman?* No, not Tyler. He loved her more than life itself. He would never be unfaithful in their marriage. Then what?

With trembling hands, she slowly opened the black velvet box and her heart sank. There, nestled in beautiful red satin, was the most elegant gold locket she had ever seen. Gold and heart-shaped, small diamonds and emeralds outlined the heart. In the middle of the heart was a larger diamond. She turned it over and engraved in small letters were these words: *Ellie, you are always in my heart. I love you! Tyler*. Well, that settled the ridiculous thought that he was having an affair. After all, it had her name on it. She felt guilty for even entertaining a thought like that. When Ellie opened the locket, she saw on the left side there were two engraved words, *Forever Yours*, and on the right side was a small picture of the two of them in their wedding attire. How had he managed to get the photo and have it made to fit in the locket? He had gone to great lengths to make sure it was perfect for her.

He had possibly meant to give it to her on their anniversary the year he was killed in Iraq and never made it home in time for them to share that special day together. Her heart was so full of love when she found the locket and yet, the pain returned reminding her of her loss. Tyler was such a special man, always thoughtful, and always trying to do anything he could to show her how happy he was with her. Oh, how she longed for his presence at that moment, wishing he could be there to put the locket around her petite neck with his tender but strong masculine hands.

With trembling fingers, she took the locket from the box and placed it around her neck, touching each stone, each link in the tiny chain, and gently rubbing her finger over the engraved words. What a treasure – not just the locket, but Tyler himself. He was the treasure God had blessed her with for so many years.

As Ellie continued with her cleaning, she repeatedly touched the gold locket, sometimes standing in front of her mirror to get a better view of the sparkling diamonds and emeralds. All these years, and she never knew it was in the closet, shoved to the far corner and probably hidden by sweaters.

After the meticulous cleaning, Ellie seemed to still have an abundance of energy and felt the need to continue to do something productive.

Proclaiming aloud, "It is still a gorgeous day and there are many hours left before dusk, so here I go – Ellie Barrett, lonely widow, but wearing a gorgeous locket." She had to snicker to herself when she realized she was going to work in her yard while sporting a very expensive piece of jewelry – a necklace that just didn't quite compliment her torn jeans, faded tee shirt, and old tennis shoes with stains and holes. She removed the precious gift and returned it to its soft nest of red satin and closed the lid.

"What in the world?" The loud roaring of a motor took Ellie by surprise as she worked in her flowers. She looked up, shaded her eyes with her hand, and saw a moving van driving past her house. *Must be new neighbors moving in!* The van slowly turned on the first street past Ellie's house and disappeared behind the trees as it made its way to a vacant house on Willow Street. Ellie remembered the Vanderson house had been empty for several months. Mr. Vanderson had passed away and soon after his death, his wife went to live with their daughter and son-in-law in another state. They were a precious couple, married for over 60 years and were inseparable. Any time Ellie saw them they were holding hands. She always hoped that she and Tyler would be like that when they got old – always romantic and deeply in love with each other. She shook her head to dismiss that thought and continued to work in her flowers.

As Ellie was cleaning up her gardening tools and getting things ready for more work tomorrow on her precious plants, the thought came to her that she should be neighborly and pack a light lunch and put it in her usual basket that she always carried to her new neighbors to welcome them to the neighborhood. Even though she couldn't see their house from where hers was located, they were still considered neighbors. She always tried to be a gracious neighbor when new folks moved in, by taking a welcoming lunch gift. She thought, *Tomorrow, yep, tomorrow, I'll prepare a lunch and meet my new neighbors.*

"Whew! All that gardening has taken a toll on my back." She moaned as she stretched and felt every muscle tingle. She knew a long hot soaking bath would take care of that issue. As she began to fill the tub, she poured in the aromatherapy liquid. The combined scent of lavender and eucalyptus filled the room. Her soft terry robe slid from her aching shoulders and she climbed into the tub. As her body slowly slid into the water, she immediately felt the warmth rise to her neck. On the edge of the tub was a small area where she always kept a few scented candles which she lit before she crawled into the tub. She smiled as she recalled a day when she was so much in need of one of these therapeutic baths after chasing the children all day. She had lit a dozen candles, turned out the bathroom light, and was soaking in her favorite bubble bath. Almost in that state of mind where you are somewhere between heaven and earth or another realm altogether, she remembered the door flying open and Tyler standing there gazing, not at her beautiful body, but at all the candles in the darkness. "Ellie," he shouted, "What on earth are you doing? You're going to burn the house down to the ground, and why didn't you answer me when I kept calling for you? I'm turning on some lights in here."

Drawn back to the hum-drum day, Ellie raised her head, which was covered in bubbles, and quickly asked, "Tyler, are you alright?" He nodded. "Are the children's body parts all intact?" Again, he nodded. "Is there any blood or deep cuts or is anyone dying?" He sheepishly let his head drop to his chest, turned around, turned off the light, quietly closed the door, and said under his breath, "I'll never understand women," to which Ellie replied, "I HEARD THAT!" Then she began to giggle, and her child-like giggles turned into a huge belly laugh. The look on Tyler's face was priceless. Her euphoric bath time was over!

Here she was, in the same tub, candles burning, and missing Tyler so much. She'd give anything if he would walk in at this very moment and caress her aching shoulders. She knew he would kiss her gently on her lips, run his fingers over her face, look deeply into her eyes, and just as the moment was becoming romantic, he would flip water in her face and then laugh. She missed those irreplaceable moments. She missed Tyler, even after all these years.

After her energizing bath, Ellie slipped into her favorite fleece-lined pajamas. It didn't matter if they had Disney characters on them. She saw them in the department store, liked them, and decided no one would ever see her in them, so why not? Her dark wet hair hung loosely over her shoulders as tiny droplets of water clung to the beautiful strands. Tyler had always loved her hair and was constantly running his fingers through it. He thought she was cutest when she had it all pulled into a ponytail with soft ringlets framing her petite face.

With her favorite TV show on low volume, she decided to make a list of the items she would need to purchase at the store in order to prepare a light lunch to take to her new neighbors. Her mind wandered as she thought about who they were, how friendly or non-friendly they might be. She was hoping the wife would be close to her age and possibly become a very good friend – one that would like to go shopping together, go to lunch at times, or find something that would be fun to do in the area of sports activities. As she thought about it, her mind took a different turn. What if the woman is too young or too old or unfriendly and wants nothing to do with her or any of the other neighbors. She decided she would wait a little while before welcoming them to the neighborhood.

Two days later, Ellie drove to the nearest grocery store and purchased all the items she needed to make a delicious lunch for the new neighbors, hoping they weren't allergic to anything she made or possibly didn't like her menu. Oh, well, she'd just take her chances with it. She had never had any complaints in the past. She hurried home, plundered for the basket she always used to take gifts, etc., to the neighbors, and began her preparation of the food.

Tyler always bragged on her chicken salad and told her no one in the world made better chicken salad. "Okay, Tyler, I'll make my "famous" chicken salad and hope the new neighbors like it as much as you did." She also had sliced baked ham, deviled eggs, sliced tomatoes, and some of her delicious homemade pickles. She even included a small loaf of her homemade sourdough bread. Her old-fashioned apple pie was included. She even included plastic forks, spoons, knives, and napkins just in case they had not unpacked all their utensils yet.

Nervously, and not knowing why, she made her way across the street and walked one block, turned left on Willow Street and recognized the house immediately. Beside the mailbox were loads of boxes and paper, and a large trash can that was overflowing with more boxes and paper. The owners were definitely getting settled in.

As Ellie walked towards the house and stepped over cardboard boxes, she noticed how unkempt the yard was. She knew the Vandersons weren't able to tend to the yard work and it had been quite a while since anything had been done to spruce up the flowerbeds or mow the lawn. She was certainly hoping the new neighbors would take an interest and make it presentable and comparable to the other homes in the neighborhood.

She lightly touched the doorbell and waited. She could hear scurrying sounds in the house and as she waited, she wondered if anyone would ever come and relieve her of the heavy basket of food. The door opened wide and there stood a young woman, probably in her late twenties or early thirties. She was quite cute with her pretty blonde hair pulled up on top of her head with strands of it striking her long, lovely neck – no wrinkles, no age spots, just a tight firm body in her jeans and tight-fitting shirt. The young woman looked at Ellie and said, "Hi, my name is Abby Monroe and we've just moved into the neighborhood."

Ellie held the basket in one hand and extended her hand to Abby and introduced herself. She held out the basket and said, "Hi, I'm Ellie Barrett and I wanted to welcome you to our neighborhood. I thought you might enjoy a small lunch while you unpack. I'm sure you are probably trying to locate all the boxes that have all the things that go in your kitchen. I included plastic utensils just in case you need them. I hope you enjoy your lunch, and I included my name, address, and phone number in case you need any help with anything. I will be happy to help."

As Abby was taking the basket from Ellie, a robust, well-formed, tall man approached the door. Ellie was speechless as she gazed at this straight-out-of-a-magazine model. He just had to be a professional model. No normal man looked like this. She thought she felt a bit of drool leaving her mouth and dripping down her chin. He had dark hair, cut short but stylish, deep blue eyes, and a tan that you only get from living at the beach. She gazed at his strong muscled arms with dark hair on them - just enough to be sexy. To top it off, he was wearing Bermuda shorts and although Ellie didn't want to stare, she glanced and noticed the muscled tan legs covered with just the right amount of hair. At this point, she felt she was blushing and needed to pull herself together in a hurry. What in the world was she thinking? Ellie Barrett was definitely having a moment that she didn't understand - not good!

The man draped his arm over Abby, displayed a gorgeous smile with beautiful even white teeth – the kind you see on TV ads. Were they all his or were they dentures or implants? Her mind was all over the place. He extended his hand and said, "Hi, I'm Steven Monroe. I see you've met Abby." By this time, Ellie was almost speechless, and she knew she must have had a dumb expression on her face. One that said, *Yep, I knew it. An older man with a younger woman, blonde hair, beautiful, and slim and equally as sexy as he is!* She couldn't wait to tell Annie. She had already described to Annie the kind of woman that older men are attracted to. Now, she could prove it.

Before Steven could say anything else, Ellie introduced herself and welcomed them to the neighborhood, shoved the basket in their hands, and left – quickly. She felt like a blithering idiot trying to make a complete sentence. She hoped he hadn't noticed how speechless she was, and she certainly hoped he had not seen her gazing at his legs, his muscles, his eyes, hair, and teeth. *Oh, my goodness*, thought Ellie, *I'm so embarrassed at my actions. I'll never be able to face them again.* She picked up her pace and thought she'd never get home, or if she could even find her house!

Ellie walked into her house, closed the door, and tried to get the picture of Steven out of her mind. After all, he was married and had an extremely cute wife. They appeared to be very devoted to each other. She certainly could not entertain the thought of how handsome he was. That just wouldn't be right, and anyway, she was still very much in love with her deceased husband. She immediately walked into the den, picked up his picture, and the old loving feelings quickly returned. She was ashamed of herself as she began to relate to Tyler what had just happened, almost asking for forgiveness from him. Nope, Ellie Barrett would not return to the new neighbor's home, even if it meant never getting her basket or dishes back. She didn't care if she never faced them again. She knew they had noticed her demeanor, especially when Steven appeared. After she left, they probably wondered, "Who was that crazy whack-o woman?" It suddenly dawned on her that she had given Abby her phone number and had offered to help in any way they needed. Oh, how she hoped they wouldn't call her. She was almost at the point of wanting to sell her house and move far away. She had never behaved in this way, not even in high school when she was beginning to have a deep interest in dating. And here she was, a grown woman, still mourning the loss of the love of her life, and another man shows up and she gets all giddy and weak-kneed. She had to get a grip and she had to do it right now!

Three

It was another beautiful morning and Ellie went through her daily routine again of getting her shower, a cup of coffee, her devotional book, and her Bible and then went out on her deck to spend some alone time with just her and God. The birds furnished the praise music. Deep into her reading, she heard a sound that brought her out of her devotional time and into the loud roar of an approaching car. It had the sound of a sports car. Tyler had always loved sports cars and he would go into great detail about them and the way different engines sounded, etc. She did recognize that this car had to be a sports car.

Straining her neck to see what was barreling down her street, she glanced at a red blur. She didn't see what kind of car it was or who was driving, but she did see that it was a hard top convertible, and the top was down. She assumed it must be a visitor to the neighborhood because she had not seen this car before. Putting it out of her mind, she returned to her passages of scripture and then her prayer time.

It was laundry day in the Barrett household and although there wasn't much of a load to do since it was only Ellie these days, she began sorting through the few items in the laundry basket. There it was again – that loud roar. It had to be the sports car returning to some house in the neighborhood. Tyler would have loved to see that car, run his hands over the beautiful red paint, and get into a very deep conversation with the owner about all the minor and major details. It was surely a "man thing."

For the first time in a long time, Ellie was bored! She missed having her children around the house and sometimes the quietness was deafening. Today was one of those days. She really wasn't in a shopping mood. She supposed she could go to the County Library, but that really didn't interest her all that much today. *How about a Hallmark movie,* Ellie thought? On second thought, she decided those movies were better watched at night while she curled up on the sofa in her Disney pajamas and indulged in a big bowl of ice cream or popcorn.

The only thing that came to her mind would be to dress in her old, ragged jeans, a tee shirt and her usual dirty tennis shoes, and work in her flower garden. That was always therapeutic for her, no matter what her mood might be for that day. Today, she just wanted to be close to the beauty of such a variety of flowers.

Donned in her gardening clothes, she made her way to the garage where she kept her gardening tools. She couldn't help but glance at all the tools and gadgets that belonged to Tyler – things that she just had not sorted through for the past five years. This was something she knew she needed to do, but not today, maybe later. She gathered everything she would need, put it all in her smaller sized wheel barrow and off she went, smiling, to her favorite place to be. Of all her beautiful array of flowers, the daisies were her favorite. Ellie always thought daisies represented happiness and joy; just a simple little flower with a friendly, happy face. She has a vast assortment of flowers, reminding her of the diversity of people in the world; each with its own size, shape, color, and fragrance. In God's world of people, each have their own talents, gifts, and skills

– all coming together to make up this wonderful earth created by the Creator.

And there it was again – that roar of the sports car engine. This time, she shaded her eyes with her hand, looked at the car and then she spotted the driver. "Oh, no," she said out loud to herself, "it's him! Mr. Gorgeous with his tanned face and arms – and legs!" Just as she was getting a bountiful eyeful, she heard the sound of the car horn and saw that muscled tan arm raised high in the air and he waved at Ellie, those gorgeous white teeth that were picture perfect, smiling at her. She couldn't have looked worse. She had been working in the dirt for about two hours and it showed! Thank goodness, he didn't stop the car. And anyway, where was Abby, his wife? She had not seen her any time at all except for that fatal day when she made an idiot of herself with her basket of goodies – like Little Red Riding Hood minus the red cape and hood. She just thought perhaps Abby was still getting their perfect house in perfect order for her perfect husband. Ellie thought, *if my drop-dead gorgeous husband was in a red sports car with the top down, you'd better believe I'd be right there beside him.* Again, out loud, she almost shouted – "ELLIE BARRETT, STOP THIS RIGHT NOW! YOU CANNOT HAVE THESE THOUGHTS ABOUT ANOTHER MAN. HE'S MARRIED, FOR GOODNESS SAKE!"

Stopping long enough to prepare a ham, lettuce, and tomato sandwich, a bag of chips and a glass of tea for her lunch, she made her way to the deck and after blessing the food, she began to devour it. She didn't realize how hungry she was. Working in the yard and her flowers usually bolstered her appetite. Ellie usually ate light meals and extremely healthy ones, except when the children came for a visit. Then she would pull out all the stops and prepare meals as if she was going to feed the entire neighborhood. And yes, it was probably very fattening food items, but she didn't care. They were her children and she wanted them to always remember "Mom's cooking."

While eating her sandwich, she noticed, in her peripheral vision, a man walking down the street past her house. Sometimes the folks in the neighborhood would walk in the early mornings or late evenings and if she was on her deck, they would always call out to her and wave. Usually, it would be couples or groups of neighbors. This was one single man making long strides. He wasn't jogging, but he was walking rather fast. As he got closer, she saw him! It was HIM! *Not again,* she thought. *What is going on? First the sports car, twice, and now he's walking near my house.* Ellie was beginning to feel a little uncomfortable. Surely, this man wasn't stalking her. She had met him and his wife a few weeks ago and they seemed happy and normal. So why had she not seen the wife since then? Why is this man, *He has a name, Ellie. Okay?* Why is Steven Monroe being seen so often near my house?'

Wondering if she had been watching too many Hallmark mysteries, she couldn't help but think it was a bit unusual that she never saw his wife. Was she stuffed in a freezer or buried in the back yard? She shuddered to even entertain that horrible thought. Putting it out of her mind for now, she continued to eat her lunch and waved as he walked by and waved to her.

It was customary in years past for everyone in the Barrett household to go to church on Sunday. Today was no exception, except it was only Ellie who would be going to church. Sometimes Sunday mornings felt so empty and lonely since the children were no longer at home.

Ellie crawled out of bed and stretched as she made her way to the bathroom. She turned on the shower and sleepily watched as the steam filled the room. Her mind wandered to the times she would be in the shower, the room all steamy, and when she got out of the shower, there would be written on the mirror in the steam, "Ellie, I love you." She knew Tyler loved her, but little things like that always seemed to reinforce that strong and faithful love. They both were always leaving little notes for each other and in the oddest places sometimes.

She recalled one time when Tyler was going to meet with some of the men from his golf team. All the wives prepared a bagged lunch for the husbands. Ellie thought it would be fun to put a note inside Tyler's lunch. She wrote a rather provocative note, the kind that's only meant to be shared between husband and wife. She had added hearts and kisses on the paper. She stuffed it inside his sandwich between the bread and the ham. She knew he would get a huge kick out of this.

Tyler and the guys had just finished nine holes of golf and they decided to take a lunch break. They gathered under one of the trees at a picnic table near the clubhouse. Each guy was talking about his lunch their wives had prepared. When Bob mentioned that his wife had made a tuna salad sandwich, Tyler's ears perked up. He loved tuna salad. Immediately the switch began. Tyler had told Bob that he would trade his ham, lettuce, and tomato sandwich for his tuna. After some thought, Bob agreed. Tyler began to woof down his sandwich, savoring the tasty tuna, when he glanced at Bob who had taken Tyler's sandwich. He was reading something and laughing. "Come on, man, share what is so funny!" grinned Tyler.

"Are you sure you want me to read this to everybody?" Something clicked and Tyler realized that Ellie had put one of her little notes in his ham, lettuce, and tomato sandwich.

"Oh, no, I know what just happened and NO, I don't want you to read that to anyone else. It was meant for me and when I get home, I'm going to tell Ellie that YOU got the note. She will probably die of embarrassment and then kill me!" Bob gave him the note, which Tyler read and even blushed a little, and they laughed till they couldn't see clearly, wiping their eyes. Bob laughingly said, "Tyler, you have a great wife with a fantastic sense of humor. She won't kill you, but she'll surely dodge being in my presence for a long time to come!" They started laughing again.

Standing in the steamy bathroom, Ellie was laughing at that incident and could still see Tyler's face when he told her that Bob had gotten her note. After she recovered from her own embarrassment, they both laughed and hugged. So many wonderful memories Ellie had of the two of them together.

So much for the recollections, it was time to get dressed for church. This was always a favorite time for Ellie and the entire family. But now, it was just Ellie and yet, she still loved attending worship services. It was her personal time to worship and praise and sing and just be happy. The church was a warm, loving and very welcoming church family and Ellie always felt at home there, especially after Tyler died and the entire church family was there for her and the children. She knew she could always depend on her pastor and the entire congregation if she ever needed anything.

Driving to church, she began to sing praise songs and was completely ready for worship by the time she arrived. Hoping she looked as happy as she felt, she walked inside and was greeted several times before finding a place to sit. Her mind was set on total worship and her heart was ready to receive the message from the pastor.

After singing several songs, it was time for the greeting. She always loved this part of the service. It was filled with kindness, love, and lots of hugs and handshakes. As she was greeting and being greeted, something happened. There seemed to be a bit of commotion near the front on the left side of the sanctuary. Ellie didn't know if someone had become ill or just what had happened. She did notice that there was a large group of women gathered in that section. Ellie almost laughed as she thought they reminded her of a group of Indians surrounding the wagons in the old Western movies. The women ranged in age from teens to probably seventies or even eighties. What in the world was going on?

BAM! There it was – the reason for the "attack." It was HIM, Steven Monroe. No wonder all the women were descending upon him like starving vultures. Who wouldn't? She pictured all these women appearing at his door with casseroles and it wasn't even a funeral. She had to chuckle at the imagined thought. But where was Abby, his wife? Something suspicious was going on and although she didn't want to play the part of a detective, she knew she just had to find out. She just didn't know how to do it.

While planning her plot, she glanced at Steven and when she did, he was looking straight at her, past all the other women who were hovering and greeting way past the greeting time of the service. When they saw each other, their eyes seemed to lock in place. She had no idea what was going through his mind, but she was trying as hard as she could to get her thoughts under control. After all, they were in church, of all places! And he is a married man!

Ellie didn't walk across the aisle to greet Steven but stayed in her place and eventually sat down. She had no idea what the pastor preached or the scripture reference. Occasionally, she would pretend to be re-positioning herself on the pew just so she could get a quick glance at Steven. What was he doing, for goodness sakes? Every time she glanced his way, he was already looking at her. She looked at her watch and wondered if this service would EVER end. She couldn't seem to get back in the worship mood or mode.

Finally, the last prayer, the hymn, and one last announcement the pastor had to make. When he finished, Ellie flew out of the sanctuary as if she was drowning in a sea of unfamiliarity. She left Steven to deal with the throngs of women who were probably lusting after him. She had heard the weather forecast for the day and it was supposed to rain, but she had no idea it would begin this early in the day. When she ran out of the church, the storm had hit and it was raining like a Biblical plague. Of course, she had no umbrella and at this point, she didn't care. She just needed to get away before he could speak to her. Sloshing through the puddles in her new Sunday heels, she got to her car, hurriedly unlocked it and scooted out of the parking lot. On her way home, and after calming down a bit, she knew she must have seemed like a genuine nut case. She usually stopped and talked to people on her way out. Well, today, perhaps they just thought she was trying to get home before the worst of the storm hit. Actually, she did see a few folks running like something was chasing them, trying to get to their cars.

Ellie was so relieved to get to her house. She parked the car in the garage and slipped into the house where she felt safe and away from her neighbor, Steven Monroe, who was seemingly wifeless. Chilled from the rain and the drop in temperature, she decided on some warm fleecy leggings and a sweatshirt. She brushed her hair and pulled it up in a ponytail, Tyler's favorite way for her to wear her hair. She missed him so much – especially today.

A bowl of soup, crackers, and a sandwich was her lunch for the day. Still feeling a bit chilled, she decided to build a fire. Tyler had always been the one to see that there was an abundant supply of wood and he had shown her the quick simple way to light a fire. She had built fires several times since he died, but she couldn't imagine why today was so difficult for her. Suddenly, the fireplace seemed big enough to roast an ox and it just all felt too much for her to handle. It was always emotionally draining for Ellie on days that were rainy or stormy. Those days seemed to bring back all the loving memories of Tyler and the days they spent together cuddled up on the sofa in front of a roaring fire, sharing their dreams and hopes for their future when he completed his time in the Marine Corps. They had such wonderful plans. She missed the giggles, the teasing, and the romance. Plain and simple – she missed Tyler.

Ellie felt the warm trickle of tears crawling down her cheeks, and soon there was a constant flow. She knew she had been holding back tears for a while and today was "release time." Crying until she was snubbing, she curled up in a tiny ball, pulled the sofa blanket over her, and waited until she was totally consumed by sleep.

The storm had passed by the time Ellie woke up and she was feeling a bit more energized. The sun was setting, and she knew it must have been getting late because she felt a few pangs of hunger. Flinging the blanket from her now very warm body, she got up, went into the kitchen, and made some hot spiced tea, ate a bowl of fresh fruit and a piece of her homemade banana bread. Not much to call it a meal, but it was just what she wanted at the moment. While nibbling on the snacks, she retrieved the remote control from the bookcase, searched the channel for a Hallmark movie – one that would make her feel all warm and fuzzy and would leave her with a mind filled with romantic thoughts. *Well,* Ellie thought, *maybe romantic thoughts aren't so great right now. I mean, who in the world would I be romantic with? Tyler isn't here.* Ellie's mind immediately found its way to Steven Monroe, which she just as quickly dismissed him from her mind. The thought kept rolling over and over in her mind – *Steven is married, and his wife is missing!* She just couldn't stand it any longer. She knew what she had to do. Tomorrow she would play the part of "Detective Ellie Barrett." She would solve this strange mystery, and no one would know what she was up to. This even sounded a bit intriguing and a bit fun at the same time. Tomorrow would be the day!

Four

Ellie found it difficult to get to sleep, knowing what she was about to do the next day. She tossed and turned and was tangled in her sheets and blanket as she planned her strategy. Sometime during the early morning hours, she finally fell asleep.

The morning was clear with blue skies, and a refreshing warm breeze. As usual, Ellie went through her daily routine and was getting dressed when the reality of what she was going to do completely wrapped itself around her, almost causing her to gasp for air. *Am I really going through with this? Am I actually going to find out if Abby is alive or snoop around to see if I can find any tell-tale signs of a struggle gone awry, possibly ending in death?* The very thought of this made her stomach churn, but she had to know the truth. "Or I could just ask him where his wife is. That would be simpler than what I'm about to do!" Ellie whispered softly to herself.

She walked outside and wandered through her yard, picking at dead leaves and flowers and mostly trying to get the nerve to step beyond her yard and into the street beside her house. "Killing time, that's what I'm doing." Ellie argued with herself over the pros and cons of stepping into a situation that she might not be able to get out of. No one knew where she'd be if she got into trouble and needed help, but what if she couldn't contact anyone if trouble was lurking. What if Steven Monroe, the specimen of perfection, wasn't so appealing while holding a gun or a knife or possibly a handkerchief soaked with chloroform? Her mind was twirling a million miles an hour with all the "what-ifs" and all the things that could go wrong. Maybe she needed to go back home and forget all this nonsense. It wasn't any of her business if his wife had left – or was stuffed in the attic or in a freezer. "Stop it, Ellie, and go home, right now!" She reprimanded herself over and over as she made her way back into her house. Her children would have a fit if they knew their Mom was toying with the idea of solving a murder case. She just wouldn't tell them. They insisted that she start a new life, and so what if she wanted to do detective work – they would sing a different tune if she did solve the case (if there is one to solve) and they'd beam with pride at her accomplishments. Nope, she would keep this to herself.

Once again, she saw him in his red sports car, zooming out of the subdivision, and still no Abby! This would be the perfect time to snoop around his yard, but how in the world would she explain herself if a neighbor saw her and inquired? She would just tell them she was there to get her basket and would explain that she had taken lunch to them when they first moved in. That's it – she had her plan in place and an explanation, or better yet, maybe she should take some of her banana bread wrapped in foil and that would be her "reason" for going there just in case someone answered the door. Either way, she had it covered.

Ellie slowly made her way towards the street where Steven and Abby lived. She had the banana bread in her trembling hands as tiny beads of perspiration covered her forehead and arms. There were no neighbors in their yards, no action in the neighborhood, so this was a good sign for Ellie. As she approached the house, her eyes were constantly searching every inch of the yard. All the paper and boxes had been removed from the day they moved in. Everything seemed neat and in place. The mailbox had been painted and had an inviting "Welcome" sign just below it. Flowers had been planted around the mailbox and a medium size rock had been painted a bright color to match the flowers. Why would they have a rock in the flower bed? Ellie wondered if they could have possibly hidden a key under it. She gently touched the rock with her toe and slid it over. There was no key, but what was that red mark on the side of the rock? Could it be blood? Was this the murder weapon? The sound of her heart pounded in her ears as she quickly turned and fled back to her house. This just wasn't her "cup of tea" and it would be best if she just stayed out of it altogether. The truth would come out eventually. Mr. Perfect might not be so perfect after all.

With all this information, true or not true, hanging over Ellie's head, she was beginning to re-think the situation. Maybe she should let someone know what she was thinking and why she was thinking this way. Let the authorities take over at this point. After mulling this over, she decided that she wasn't going to get involved in it. She told herself that there really wasn't any evidence that a crime had been committed. Maybe Abby was away visiting relatives or on a business trip. After all, Steven had been in church so he couldn't be all that bad; however, it could be a cover-up for his crime.

Ellie knew she had to quit thinking about this and make an effort to leave it alone and get back to her life – her very boring life. Well, it was exciting for a short while as she was playing the part of "Detective Ellie Barrett." Tyler would skin her alive if he knew she was even considering putting herself in danger. No, she was through with it all, but she was hoping she wouldn't see Steven again at church, in his red sports car, or at the grocery store or anyplace at all.

Another gorgeous day and Ellie sat on her deck drinking her coffee and spending some worship time with God. She was feeling on top of the world and decided it was time to extend that feeling of intimacy with her Heavenly Father and step into her own world of beauty – her flower garden. As she gathered her gardening tools once again, she couldn't help but thank God again for the beauty of nature and His handiwork in all of it.

As Ellie was pruning and humming at the same time, she saw what she had always dreaded. Nestled in the grass and between the mulch and flowers was a long black snake. In her opinion, every snake was poisonous, and she was now faced with what to do. Tyler would have known what to do and if he ever saw one, he would take care of the situation and later tell Ellie about it. "But Tyler isn't here," Ellie said to herself. "What am I supposed to do? I can't kill this huge snake by myself." She began to pray as the hairs began to stand up on her body. She was extremely afraid at this point, and she could feel the tears building up in her eyes. "Please, God, help me. Send someone who can help me. I can't do this by myself!"

Isn't it amazing how God works sometimes? In the midst of a situation that seems hopeless, He always steps in and solves it. Today was no exception. God knew Ellie was in distress and He was there to help.

Gazing with her fingers over her eyes and only peeking out through the small openings between her fingers, she eyed the snake that was just enjoying the warm sunshine and not moving at all. Her mind was totally on this bigger-than-life snake when she heard singing. She knew it wasn't coming from the snake, but who? She glanced over her shoulder, not wanting to let the snake out of her sight, and there he was! He always seemed to show up at odd times. Steven Monroe was walking down the street at a quick pace and singing or humming. Had God sent her help for her situation? She couldn't scream to him to come to her rescue, but God had already worked all of that out as Steven slowly walked towards her and asked if everything was okay. Her expression was a dead give-away that she was in distress.

Immediately Ellie felt fear creeping through her body with him so close and yet, she felt relief. The would-be possible murderer on one side and the gigantic snake on the other side. She was caught in the middle. She "quietly" yelled and motioned to him to stay there because there was a huge snake in her flower bed, and she didn't know what to do. Who was she more afraid of, the snake or Steven Monroe, potential wife-killer? He continued to walk towards her smiling with that gorgeous mouth. She nervously stood on her tip-toes and asked him to stay away, but he continued to get closer. She wanted to jump up and down, but her legs wouldn't cooperate.

"Ellie, do you have any tools in your garage?" She nodded. "Please, quickly and quietly find a shovel or a hoe and bring it to me. I'll take care of this for you." Ellie ran like her pants were on fire. She was on a mission – a mission to find a tool that Steven could use. As she entered her garage, she glanced around at all of Tyler's tools so neatly spaced and hung on nails, all out of her reach. *Now what?* she thought. Tyler was tall and never thinking that Ellie would need to use any of his tools, he had hung them at his own height, but there it was….just like God to provide, isn't it? Leaning against the wall in the corner was a shovel. She shouted, "Thank You, God."

Running with the shovel in her hands, Ellie stood at a distance and waited for Steven to approach her. She wasn't about to get near that horrible snake. She didn't even want to look at it. Steven took the shovel and slowly and quietly inched his way to the totally resting snake. He stood there and Ellie was about to have a flying fit. "Steven, what are you doing? What is the snake doing? Why aren't you killing it?"

"Come here, Ellie. I want you to see this."

"Are you crazy?" yelled Ellie. "I am most certainly NOT going to go over there and look at a snake! Now please kill it and get it out of my flowers and out of my sight – and HURRY!" Ellie was frantic. Steven could see how upset she was, but still he insisted. At this point, Ellie was dancing from one foot to the other and shaking her arms and hands in the air.

"Ellie, do you trust me?"

BAM, there it was. Trust him, knowing what she thought she knew about his missing wife – trust him? Was he crazy? "I don't know if I trust you or not, Steven, I don't even know you."

"I wouldn't let anything hurt you and I want you to come and see this before I dispose of it." Ellie was wondering why he was so adamant about her seeing this horrible black snake.

Trembling with fear of so many things, she slowly made her way, inch by inch. She kept her eyes on Steven as he had the shovel on or under the snake. This was by far the most horrible situation she had been in since Tyler's death. As she got closer, Steven lifted the shovel with the snake hanging limply over it. Ellie screamed, "STOP IT, STEVEN. GET RID OF IT, PLEASE, HURRY. I CAN'T STAND TO LOOK AT IT." She was almost in tears when Steven began to laugh.

This man is incorrigible, she thought. He was laughing while she was almost hysterical with fear. She stopped dead in her tracks as she glanced at the dangling snake.

"Ellie, your huge poisonous snake is nothing more than an old black dry-rotted garden hose. It has probably been here for years, and you just didn't notice it. Please come here so you will know I'm telling you the truth." She made her way closer to Steven and the "snake" and then as she could feel her heart rate begin to slow, she broke out in a huge grin and then one of her old-fashioned belly laughs. They both howled in laughter and amusement as the garden hose was laid to rest in the garbage can. Ellie told Steven she would just have to be present when the garbage truck came by for pick-up. She wanted to see their reaction when they dumped the trash can and the "snake of the century" fell on them. There was Ellie's crazy sense of humor, seemingly returning after so many years.

After her knight in shining armor had come to her rescue, she felt that she should at least invite him to sit on the deck with her and have a glass of her freshly made lemonade. He accepted and while he waited for her to return with the refreshing drink, she looked around her neat yard, the gorgeous flowers, minus the snake, and was extremely impressed with her expertise in making it all so beautiful.

She returned with the lemonade and slices of her scrumptious banana bread, still a bit warm from the morning's baking. She didn't realize how hungry she was until she was seated next to someone who would enjoy the snack with her. She was so used to eating alone and this seemed really soothing to her. As they sat in a snippet of silence, Ellie wondered if she should bring up her suspicions. With sweaty palms, she decided to just come right out with her questions. At least they were out in the open in case he became violent, and she could scream for help.

"Steven, I've noticed you driving in and out of the neighborhood and you are always alone. And then on Sunday, you were in church, and you were alone. Is your wife alright? I mean, I haven't seen her since the day I took lunch to you, and I was just wondering if she is ill or possibly out of town." There, she said it. Now, what would he say or do?

"My WIFE? Ellie, my wife passed away several years ago. You are probably referring to Abby. She's my daughter and she was helping me get moved in and settled. She's a busy pediatrician in a nearby town but took some time off to help me." He started to laugh, showing off those gorgeous teeth and full smooth lips. His eyes sparkled.

Guilt swept over Ellie as she thought about the horrible things she had suspected that Steven had done. In her heart she knew he couldn't have been that type of person, but it all seemed so possible. Yes, she knew at this point that she had been watching too many Hallmark mysteries. She needed to make a change.

Letting the thoughts of potential crimes being committed slip from her mind, she relaxed, and they had a wonderful conversation, sharing their stories of loss. She was beginning to see a wonderful, caring, and sensitive man; one who she hoped would become a good friend – not just to kill make-believe snakes, but one she felt comfortable with if she should ever need help with anything. Their conversation went on for hours until they realized the sun was beginning to set and they had been so wrapped up in this new friendship that they didn't even notice.

Thanking him profusely for coming to her rescue, she walked him to the steps on the deck. He smiled that heart-stopping smile and thanked her for the lemonade and banana bread and especially for the conversation. A new friendship was formed, and Ellie couldn't have been more excited. She just wondered if Steven felt the same way.

Gathering up the dishes, she sauntered into the house and felt a rising elatedness– something she had not felt since Tyler's death.

Walking down the hallway to her bedroom, she glanced at herself in the mirror. Shock overtook her as she wondered who was staring back at her. She had never seen herself look so pathetic. No makeup, hair a total mess, and look at her clothes! There was that old, faded tee shirt with a few rips in it, her cutoff jeans that were just as ragged and faded and those horrible tennis shoes full of holes and stains and dirt. Could she have looked any worse?

Emphatically, NO! Embarrassment set in quickly as she thought about Steven in his light blue golf shirt, navy shorts and spotless white canvass shoes which covered his probably beautiful feet and that tan – oh, what a gorgeous tan he had, framed by his dark hair and deep blue eyes. *Ellie Barrett, what in the world are you doing? Stop this nonsense right now.* She knew she would have to take more time with her looks just in case…..

The evening was uneventful for Ellie. She put a frozen dinner in the microwave, prepared her favorite hot tea and settled on the sofa to eat alone – again. Her mind wandered to her children, wondering what they were doing tonight. She was so blessed to have such wonderful and caring children. She would love to talk to them every single day or night but knew they had lives of their own. She also knew they would come running to her rescue if there was a need – like killing a black garden hose. She started to laugh at the craziness of the day, and she recalled the muscled arms of Steven as he "killed" the life-threatening snake. She kept laughing at all of it and as she laughed, she realized it had been a very long time since she had laughed and enjoyed a man's company - not since Tyler.

In between bites of her so-called dinner, she also wondered what Annie and Mark would say if they knew she was even entertaining the thought of another man. Would they be shocked, disappointed, rebellious to the thought, or would they be happy for their mom who was beginning to emerge from her five year old cocoon of sadness and loneliness? Maybe she would call them soon and get their take on the idea. But for tonight, it was just Ellie and Hallmark, but this time, it wasn't a mystery, it was a romance movie.

Five

Ellie woke up all tangled in her sheets and blankets after a fitful night of sleep. She felt fine physically, but her mind was filled with thoughts, ideas, plans, and everything was scrambling like morning eggs. Her mind quickly raced to Steven Monroe and the day they had spent on her deck. "This just isn't working," said Ellie as she stared at herself in the bathroom mirror. "I have to talk to someone about all of this." Pastor Jim came to her mind. Of course, she could and would talk to him. He had been her pastor for years, had performed the wedding ceremony for her and Tyler and had been present for her children's births. He was the perfect person to talk to, knowing it would all be confidential. The decision was made – she felt better already.

Was everything greener and brighter and happier? Ellie was feeling very optimistic about her situation as she drove down the tree-lined streets and noticed the beauty of hanging baskets, flowers along the sidewalks in town and just a sweet presence of God.

She drove into the church parking lot and sat still for a few minutes trying to gather her thoughts before dumping them all on Pastor Jim's desk. *'It's now or never,'* she thought. Opening the car door and stepping out onto the pavement, she straightened her blouse and held her shoulders back and paraded into the building, still not knowing for sure just what to say or how to say it. Then it dawned on her that she had not called to make an appointment to see the pastor. He was such a busy man, always ministering to people. She greeted Sally, the church secretary, and asked if she could make an appointment to see Pastor Jim. At that very moment, he walked in the front office and gave Ellie one of those sweet pastoral hugs. She told him she was making an appointment to see him, but he gently led her into his office while telling her he always had time for her. *What a wonderful pastor*, she thought. But then she thought that possibly he would look at her in a different light if she told him why she was there.

"Ellie, you look radiant today. What's going on with you these days? I didn't get an opportunity to speak to you at church so I'm glad you're here." They made small talk about the children, the weather, the upcoming church-wide event, and other little items. She was skirting the issue and she knew it. *Okay, Ellie, it's SHOW TIME*, she thought.

"Pastor Jim, I'm here because I have questions that I need answers to. I know you are aware that Tyler has been gone for five years and my whole world revolved around him and the children."

Pastor Jim knew where this conversation was headed, but he just nodded and let her talk. He knew she needed to get it all out of her system and he was so glad she came to him. Together, they would find answers, and all based on God's Word.

"I hardly know where to begin except to tell you how much I love Tyler and how much I miss him. The children have mentioned to me many times that I need to begin a new life, but I can't forget about Tyler or our marriage that was so beautifully filled with love. I can't just push him aside like unwashed laundry. He was my life! Please tell me what you think. Tell me if I should begin again. Should I just forget about Tyler and what we shared? I just can't do that, but I do know that I need to get out of my comfort zone, my safe place, and do things other than watch TV, go to church, work in my flowers, and go to the grocery store. Please, Pastor Jim, tell me what to do. I feel like I'd be unfaithful to Tyler if I should ever decide to date again, which I don't want to do simply because I don't know how to begin again. I don't know how to date." She put her head down briefly on his desk and mumbled, "Oh, this is such a mess and it's just way too hard to do." *Breathe, Ellie, breathe!* her mind kept telling her. She knew she had just dumped everything on Pastor Jim and probably did it without even taking a breath – it just all came rolling out.

Pastor Jim lightly touched her head, and she sat up. He could see the stress and fear in her eyes and expression. Before he could say anything, she blurted out about the new man in her neighborhood, the one that visited the church on Sunday, and she also let it slip that she thought he might have been a murderer. Pastor Jim's eyebrows lifted, eyes widened, and he sat straight up in his chair. "Ellie Barrett, what in this world made you think he was a murderer?" She had come too far now so she might as well finish. She lowered her voice and glanced around the room and then relayed the entire story of her shenanigans of how to solve the mystery. Pastor Jim couldn't help but laugh and she realized how silly it all sounded which made her double over in laughter.

"Okay, Ellie, let's talk about the real issues. You've met Steven Monroe and you find him attractive. Am I right so far?" She sheepishly nodded, somewhat embarrassed at hearing someone else say it. "I know Steven and he is a wonderful Christian man who was devoted to his wife during her illness. He has been widowed for several years, just like you. And yes, he is an attractive man. I think that was evident when he came to church and was bombarded by all the single women there." They both laughed.

"Ellie, God has been perfectly clear in His Word about marriage. You are both widowed, and God can bring others into your lives to make you happy again. There is absolutely nothing wrong with you dating again and possibly opening yourself up to a future with someone else. Don't shut Steven, or any other man you might be interested in, out of your life. Give yourself a chance to explore the idea of dating and having some fun. God will lead you and He will make it clear to you just exactly what you need to do or not do. You have a strong faith, Ellie, and I know you will be fine. Continue to read and study the Bible. I'm always available to listen or help in any way." They spent time sharing scriptures and discussing them. Pastor Jim had prayer with Ellie and when she left, a sense of relief had washed over her. Now, it was time to tell the children.

After leaving the church office, she sat in her car for a few minutes contemplating how she would tell the children. She picked up her cell phone and stared at the screen. She knew she wanted to call the children and tell them of her latest news. Should she call Annie first or maybe Mark would be better. No, she wouldn't call either of them. No, she knew she had to tell them. Actually, there wasn't anything to tell them. What would she say? "Hello. I have a new neighbor. Tell me about your day." *Oh, that is so dumb*, Ellie thought. *Just tell them. Maybe they will be happy for you.*

With trembling fingers, she dialed Annie's office number. In her sweet and Southern accent, she heard her daughter say, "Good Morning, this is Annie Barrett. How may I help you?"

"Hi, Annie, it's your Mom." Excited to hear her mother's voice, she immediately sat back in her chair and said, "Mom, it's so good to hear from you. What's going on?" Silence on Ellie's end of the line. "Mom, are you there? Is something wrong?" A strong awareness that she was going to be hit with some bad news, Annie stood up, walked to the nearby office window and said, "Mom, whatever it is, tell me. We can fix it."

Ellie regained her composure and told Ellie nothing was wrong and that she missed her and Mark. She asked her if she could come to dinner on Friday evening and that she would call Mark to see if he could be there, too. Relieved, Annie agreed to be there, and she felt sure Mark would be available, too. They made small talk and laughed about the little things they had been experiencing. Ellie loved her children and could hardly wait to see them. She made the call to Mark, and he was equally excited about his Mom's home-cooking. It all made her smile. Now, she had to try to figure out just how she would break the news to them. Not that there was really any news, but she wanted them to know her plans to try to "begin again." She hoped they would be happy for her. She needed reinforcement from her children.

Ellie had not seen Steven drive through the neighborhood since the fateful "snake day." It made her feel a bit uneasy that possibly he was avoiding her. He knew she spent a lot of time in her flower garden and maybe he just didn't want to have to deal with whatever this was between them. Not seeing her would make it easier for him. She hoped she had not made a total idiot of herself or maybe it was her appearance that day. After all, she didn't rate right on up there with the "Top 10 Best Dressed Women." Her mind was racing with all sorts of reasons why she had not seen him. For the first time, she realized she actually missed seeing him. Whoa! Where was this coming from? She was overwhelmed by a feeling of warmth and happiness that amazed her. It had been a long time since she felt this way. It finally dawned on her, and she was hesitant, but willing, to admit – she had feelings for Steven Monroe.

It was Friday and Annie and Mark would soon be arriving. Ellie had mixed emotions about the news she would be sharing with them. Part of Ellie knew there was really nothing to tell, but another part wanted to tell them all about him. She wasn't sure how to begin, so she began to prepare her heart by praying – asking God for wisdom and guidance and that the children would be accepting of her beginning a new life; well, at least a life of starting to date. She had no idea what the future would hold, but she did know that God held her future and she would trust Him with it.

Out of nervousness, Ellie prepared enough food to feed the entire neighborhood. She always cooked or baked when she was antsy and today was no exception. She also knew that anything she prepared, they would devour it and take leftovers home with them.

She heard the roar of an engine in the driveway and recognized it as Mark's car. Shortly after, Annie was there. Everyone exchanged hugs and Ellie was thrilled to have her children with her, like old times. The house was filled with delightful mouth-watering aromas. One would have thought it was Thanksgiving or Christmas with such a spread of food.

Chattering and sometimes all talking at once, they shared the things that were going on in their lives. Ellie loved hearing them talk and she basked in the warmth of their conversations and laughter. After dinner, Annie helped her mother clear the table, put away the food and package up lots of leftovers for her and Mark to take with them. The kitchen, now cleaned, and a pot of coffee brewing, Ellie sat down in the den, propped her feet on the coffee table and sat there speechless, not knowing how to begin.

"Okay, Mom, out with it. We know you invited us here because you have something you want to talk about, and when we saw the feast you prepared, we knew for sure you had something on your mind. You always cook like that when you're bothered by something. So here we are. Let's hear it."

"Such perceptive children I have raised," Ellie laughed. "Yes, you are right; there is something I want to discuss with you." This was more difficult than Ellie had imagined, and her heart rate kicked up a notch or two. "I know you both have expressed your strong desire for me to begin a new life, as you put it. You think I don't do anything exciting, and I know you are concerned about me and my future. I'm not old and I don't rank up there with the Dinosaurs so I've been giving a lot of thought to what you have both been saying."

"Oh, Mom, who is he? What's his name? Tell me all about him." Annie was the romantic in the family and loved a good love story. Mark was more concerned with his mom's happiness and care and security.

Annie blurted out, "When can we meet him? Does he have children? Is he cute? Where does he live? How did you meet?" Ellie was bombarded with questions that she knew Annie would ask but wasn't sure if she wanted to answer all of them right now.

Mark was quiet. Finally, he looked at his mom and said, "Mom, do you love him and does he love you? Is he a Christian and is he kind and caring and does he have room in his heart for Annie and me….and Dad?"

Quickly, Ellie told them that she had not even been on a date so how in the world could she even speak of love. All she wanted them to know was that she was taking their advice and opening herself up to the possibilities of dating, and she wanted to know how they felt about it. She also wanted them to know that she still loved Tyler with all her heart, and she wasn't sure anyone else could or would ever take his place. "This is only the first step," she told them. "I'm willing to give it a try although I'm not sure how to begin. I do know that I will NEVER love anyone like I loved your father."

Annie spoke up, "Mom, never say never! You don't know what God has planned for your life." She hugged her Mom and expressed her approval. Mark sat motionless, uncertainty plastered all over his face. Ellie wasn't sure if he would be so open with his approval, or disapproval, as Annie had been.

That's all she wanted them to know at this point. Maybe eventually, she would share how they met, the snake incident, and the would-be-murder mystery. She knew they would howl with laughter at that one – but not tonight. This night was for them to all enjoy being together as a family, kicking off their shoes, wrapping up in a blanket by the fire and loving each other. Thoughts of Steven crawled through her mind, and she sheepishly wished he was there, too.

It was almost midnight when the three of them began to wind down from all the conversation and laughter. This had been an evening that Ellie had needed for a long time and as she looked at her children, she realized just how much they resembled Tyler. Annie had her mother's facial features and Mark had his father's muscular frame. His mannerisms were the spitting image of Tyler. She couldn't stop gazing at them and thinking of Tyler when Annie spoke up. "Mom, why do you keep looking at Mark and me and what in the world is going through your mind?"

Ellie smiled and told them about her thoughts about them and how much they resembled their father. It was almost like having him there in the room with them, which brought comfort to Ellie.

Rising from the soft cushiony sofa, and realizing the time of night, they both decided it would be best if they spent the night and left the next morning, which of course, thrilled Ellie to know her children were in the house all night. It even eased her mind and she felt safe. She was already thinking of the huge breakfast she would prepare for them before they had to leave.

Nestled in her bed and snuggling up to Tyler's pillow, she began to let her thoughts run loose and immediately Steven Monroe was there, in her mind, possibly in her heart. Even though Ellie thought this would be a night of rest, knowing her children were down the hall in their own rooms, she couldn't find the sleep she desired. She tossed, turned, struggled with the sheets and blanket, and every time she would close her eyes, he was there – Steven Monroe, with his perfect physique, beautiful tan, eye-blinding white teeth, and a warm smile that would melt the snow and ice in Antarctica. His laughter was contagious and the very fact that he would sit and listen to Ellie ramble on and on about practically nothing for hours, intrigued her. He always seemed to truly be interested in anything she said. Even Pastor Jim said he was a fine Christian man with a heart of gold. Ellie thought, *If all this is true, then why am I so afraid to take a chance? What would Tyler think if he knew I was contemplating dating again? Would he be in favor of it, or would he be devastated at the thought of me being with another man?*

Ellie crawled out from under the twisted sheets and blanket and knelt beside the bed – her side of the bed. She quickly removed the pillow from the bed and placed it under her knees. She knew this was going to be a long night and a long prayer, but she had to allow God to be involved in the decisions she would be making. As long as she followed His lead, she knew everything would fall into place at the right time and in the right way. She began to lift her petitions to the throne of God.

It was six o'clock when Ellie gazed blurry-eyed at the clock next to the bed. Her first thought was why she was on the floor, but then she quickly remembered last night. She was still next to her bed with her head on the pillow that had been under her knees when she began to pray. At some point, she had reached for the sheet and blanket and managed to pull it from the bed and had wrapped herself in it, resembling a cocoon. As she began to unravel herself from the bed coverings, she stood, stretched, and suddenly felt the pain of being on the floor in a balled-up position for hours. "Ellie Barrett, you are not the spring chicken you once were and you cannot sleep like this again," she spoke aloud.

Getting her thoughts and mind in some sort of order, she realized she smelled coffee brewing and then remembered Annie and Mark were still here and probably had already pulled the Cheerios from the cabinet and were devouring them. She put on her robe and carefully and stiffly walked to the kitchen where she was greeted by her two precious adult children.

"Good morning, Mom." Annie was always so cheerful when she got up in the mornings and Ellie remembered all the school days when Annie would be bouncing around in the den, ready for school. Mark was, on the other hand, slow-moving and it always took a few minutes before he even knew where he was. However, this morning, they were both sitting at the breakfast table, Cheerios in their bowls and they were smiling at her.

"Okay, what's going on in here, and why are you grinning like you've just won the lottery?" Ellie knew they were conjuring up something and she wasn't quite sure if it was something she was going to agree with. Nevertheless, she would listen to their "plan." She stared at them while Annie poured a cup of coffee for her.

"Again, what's going on? I know you two are plotting and I want to know what it is." By this time, Ellie was grinning right along with them, but she was still anxiously wondering what was going on between the two of them.

Bouncing up from the table and pulling out a chair for her mom, Annie spoke first. "Now, Mom, don't say anything until you've heard all we have to say. Promise?" Ellie promised, reluctantly. *Maybe I'd better have my coffee black and very strong in order to hear what I'm about to hear,* Ellie thought.

"Mark and I have discussed this, and we think it would be a good idea if the three of us go out to dinner one evening soon and invite Steven Monroe." Ellie was taking a gulp of her coffee when she sputtered, and it came flying out of her mouth.

"What on earth are you talking about? I haven't even gone out with him on a date and you are wanting the three of us to invite him to dinner and do what, screen him, ask a million questions, give him the once over? Oh, no, I'm not about to do that. Anyway, he might not be interested in me at all and would be horrified at the thought of making his grand entrance in the presence of my children, who, by the way, he has never met!" Ellie gained her composure and immediately thanked them for caring about her, but she did let them know that she was not ready for any of this. Actually, she wasn't even sure if she wanted to date again. She wondered if there was a book entitled "Dating for Dummies." Perhaps she would do a little research on that topic.

Annie and Mark wouldn't take "no" for an answer and they explained their reasons for wanting her to be happy again and to be able to enjoy the fun side of life like she and Tyler used to do.

"Mom, we believe Dad would want you to date and find someone who would make you happy; someone who would take care of you and love you just as much as he did." Ellie knew they were right, and their explanation rocked her world; she asked herself that a million times. Would Tyler want this for her?

Ellie smiled, took their hands in hers, and told them how much she loved them, how much she loved their dad, and she realized that he would not want her sad or lonely, or crying unnecessarily. She told them all the things that she had been feeling for their dad and also for Steven, but she also told them that she wasn't sure about Steven's feelings for her, other than just a great friendship. However, she did promise them that she would think about it, pray about it, and would let God take the lead in all of it. She ended their conversation by saying, "If it's meant to be and if it's God's will for my life, then it will happen in His time, not mine, yours, or Steven's – only in God's time."

Mark and Annie looked at each other and then at their mother. "Okay, Mom, that's fair enough, but we want you to know that we are also going to be praying about all of this with you. Will you promise us that when you get an answer, you will let us know?"

"Absolutely! You will be the first to know – after I've told your dad." Laughter filled the breakfast room and today Ellie's Cheerios seemed a bit sweeter and crunchier, the room seemed brighter, and Ellie's heart felt as if it would explode with excitement and joy. A new beginning for Ellie Barrett!

Now what? thought Ellie. She was mulling over the conversation that she and her children had the night before and the next morning. She was beginning to get confused and somewhat aggravated with herself over all this "hoopla" about dating again. *How should she approach it? How should she approach Steven, or should she wait for him to make the first move? And if he did bring up the subject of going out on a date, what would she say?* All these thoughts kept racing through her already confused mind. *Maybe it would just be easier if I just forgot about all of it – just continue my life as I have been for the past five years; working in my flower garden, watching Hallmark movies, going to church and the grocery store.* Even as Ellie was thinking all of this, it all actually seemed rather boring. She knew in her heart that it was time to make a change and a time to look forward to a new future – with or without Steven Monroe. Yet, deep in her heart and mind, that little nudge kept saying, *preferably WITH Steven Monroe.*

Ellie spent the remainder of the morning and early afternoon preparing her flower garden for the fall season. There was a brisk chill in the air, although it wasn't time for heavy coats, and she wasn't sure if it was the coolness of the air or if the tiny shivers were from anticipation that Steven might walk by her house. As she dug up the old flowers and began to till the soil in preparation for the fall plants, she kept glancing toward the street hoping to see him, but he never came her way. She listened for the roar of the engine of his sports car, but all was silent. She was disappointed. She had dressed in clean jeans and a cute long-sleeved blouse, washed and styled her hair, and had on makeup – just in case! But as she continued to work without getting completely submerged in dirt, she realized that he wasn't going to be there.

After putting her gardening tools away and throwing away the empty bag of mulch, she began her trek to her steps and deck. Shoulders drooping and her head hung a little lower, she pictured herself as a throw-away rag doll; one that no one wanted any longer, heading towards the thrift store, or worse, the trash dump. Disappointment made her heart hurt and she fought the tears that wanted to splash down her cheeks. She just wanted to rush into her house, close the blinds, turn off all the lights, and just sit and cry or yell or whatever it would take to make her feel better.

As she entered the house, she immediately went to the den where Tyler's picture rested on the mantel. Picking it up and holding it close to her heart, she let the tears flow as she limply sat on the sofa. Pulling the soft blanket over her, she curled up in a fetal position and held tightly to the picture. Thoughts of her wonderful husband filled her mind, and she cried harder. In her mind, she began to pray. *God, why am I feeling like this? I don't know what to do. If you want me to begin a new life and begin to date again, then You will have to make it happen. I'm exhausted from all this "new life again" stuff. Tyler was and still is my life. Please help me, God, know what to do.*

And just as God always does, he calmed her, gave her a peaceful nap, and watched over His child with love.

Ellie was peacefully sleeping when the sudden sound of her cell phone ringing woke her. Still a bit groggy, she answered it and tried to sound "chipper" and not half asleep.

"Hello." Silence – nothing – just soft breathing. Ellie was a little disturbed at this "nothingness" on the phone and was about to hang up when she heard a soft voice say, "Hi, Ellie. This is Steven Monroe." She bolted from the sofa, began to straighten her mussed hair (as if he could see her!) and said, "Hi, Steven, it's nice to hear from you." *Oh, my goodness, how corny do I sound?* she thought.

Both were at a loss for words, so Ellie began a conversation asking how he was doing, how she had not seen him lately, and if he had been to the grocery store... *WHAT? Ellie, are you a total idiot? Why would you ask him if he'd been to the grocery store? What is wrong with you?* thought Ellie.

Steven laughed and asked her if she had been tormented by any other snakes in her flower garden. The conversation took off and before long they were laughing and joking with each other – feeling totally comfortable in their conversations.

Ellie hadn't even realized that while they were talking, she had gone into the kitchen, made herself a cup of her favorite spiced tea, fixed a bowl of fresh fruit, and had begun to slice a piece of her banana bread. All of this was interspersed with laughter and questions and just simple fun conversation.

Two hours later, they said their good-byes and Ellie was on top of the world! It had been ages since she had felt like a teenager with a high school crush on the star football player. She was giddy with excitement and wished she could call her children, but this wasn't the right time for that. She just wanted to take some time and bask in the realization that she was now ready to begin a new life of dating and test the waters to see what would happen. She also wondered if he would call again and when and if he would possibly ask her out on a date. That thought made her stop in her tracks. A date? A real date? Like, going out in a car to a place in public kind of date? She grinned and then laughed.

It had been a week since Ellie had heard from Steven and she was beginning to wonder if she had just dreamed all this. Had he really called and had they really talked for two hours? She kept wishing her phone would ring and she would hear his deep voice. She knew she wouldn't call him – not that it would be wrong to do that, but her parents were from the "old school" and had taught her it was never the right thing to do for a girl to call a boy! *Sorry, Mom and Dad, but I think it's time for me to change a little bit of my thinking.* The thought of this and of a million other things they had taught her began to rush through her mind as she wondered what they would think if they knew she was anticipating dating again. Surely, they would be happy for her and want her to have a new and happy life, wouldn't they? Of course, they would, Ellie tried to convince herself.

The day was almost over and still Ellie had not heard from Steven. With sweaty palms, dry mouth, and a heart that pounded like a sledgehammer, she walked over to her cell phone. She stared at it as if it was going to bite her and spew venom from it. Slowly, she picked it up, stared at the keypad, and then threw it on the sofa. "I can't do this. What if he thinks I'm being too forward and assuming? What if he doesn't want to talk to me? What if another woman answers the phone?" She was on a tangent with the "what-if" game.

"Ellie, get control of yourself! It's just a phone call to a friend, for goodness sakes." It seemed lately she was having several of these personal conversations with herself. She walked to the sofa, carefully picked up the cell phone and this time, she dialed Steven Monroe's number. As it rang, she yelled out loud, "Oh, gosh, oh, gosh, it's ringing!" She thought about hanging up when a strong and rather sexy voice said, "Hi, Ellie." *What? How did he know it was me? she thought.* It quickly dawned on her strained brain that he had programmed her number in his phone, so her name popped up on the screen. *Duh!* she thought.

She had never been a person who had to grasp for words, but tonight, she won the crown for silence. Finally, she spoke and asked how he was and about his day, but then was at a total loss as to what to say next. She told him that it was definitely not her nature to be calling men. She tapped herself against her head and thought how THAT sounded! Could it get any worse? Well, she was in it now and must continue. Trying to dig herself out of a very deep hole, she let the words flow about her children's desire for her life and how she was terrified of beginning again. He responded in a similar manner about his daughter wanting the same for him and the difficulty he had with starting over.

Not two hours, but three, had passed this time on the phone together and neither of them seemed to tire of talking and listening to each other, their conversations filled with laughter and fun. And then it happened!

"Ellie, would you like to go out to dinner with me on Friday night?" Silence. "Ellie, are you there? Hello?" Still silence. For what seemed like an eternity, Ellie finally answered him. "Yes." She didn't know what else to say at that point. She could hear the excitement in his voice as he told her he'd be at her house at six o'clock on Friday night and would take her to *"Maison de Bonne Nourriture"*, a French restaurant known for its outstanding cuisine. The name of the restaurant simply means, "House of Good Food." Ellie had never been there but had read rave reviews about it and she was already feeling the excitement rising in her.

Then it hit her – what would she wear to a fancy French restaurant? This was the time to call in the "forces." She would call Annie and tell her the news and she knew that Annie would know exactly what one wears to a fancy French restaurant – on a first date! She had only four days to select something to wear. It had to be just exactly the right dress and shoes to match. She felt the same way when she was in high school, and Tyler had asked her to the

Senior Prom. *Oh, no….Tyler!* It all came rushing back to her – would he agree with her going to dinner with another man? Would he be hurt knowing she was about to embark upon a new life of dating? Maybe this is all wrong and maybe she should call Steven back and break the date. No, she couldn't disappoint him like that, and she didn't want to appear as a scared teenager on a first date. *I'll be fine. It will all be fine.* She kept telling herself all these things and soon she was breathing normally again as the excitement returned. She still needed to call Annie and she knew they would giggle and laugh and make plans to go shopping. A mother/daughter day would be fun and perhaps Annie could give her some "tips" on how to make the first date interesting and leave him with a strong desire to see her again.

Ellie jumped and danced around the den, twirling, and dipping and finally flopping on the sofa – "This is going to be so much fun," Ellie yelled as she kicked her feet in the air in a childlike manner.

Later that evening as Ellie prepared her nighttime snack and was getting settled on the sofa, she decided to make the call to Annie and break the earth-shattering news that she was going on a date. Feeling a bit nervous, she toyed with the cell phone, nibbled on her crackers and cheese, laid the cell phone on the table, ate some more crackers and cheese, and then finally made the call.

"Hi Mom," said Annie in her usual cheerful voice. "What's up?" Ellie never really understood that term but figured it must have meant what was she doing. She cleared her throat, took a deep breath, and quickly rolled out the words, "I have a date." She knew the neighbors a block away could hear the happy scream from Annie.

"Hallelujah! Mom, that's great and I already know who the lucky man is. It's Steven Monroe, isn't it?" Ellie could feel a huge grin spreading across her already blushing face. "Yes, it is, and I'm already a nervous wreck. Annie, I need your help in getting just the right dress and shoes to wear." She relayed all the information to Annie, who, by the way, was jumping and dancing with excitement all over her den. She wanted the two of them to go shopping for an outfit and all the accessories – this date night had to be perfect.

They agreed they would meet the next day, have lunch together, and then go shopping. Both of them giggling and acting like teenagers, it was an exciting night for them to make plans for Ellie to start her new journey – one that she wasn't sure she was completely ready for, but she was willing to try. She also wondered if Steven was as excited and nervous as she was. Somehow, she couldn't picture him jumping and dancing all around his den with the excitement that she was feeling. Nope, not Steven. He was probably more laid back and calm – maybe!

Ellie ran to her bedroom and began rummaging through her closet. She wasn't exactly sure why because she knew she and Annie were going shopping for the perfect dress. *It's just nerves,* she thought. As she stood in her huge closet, she looked at all the clothes hanging and realized she had not bought anything new for herself in ages. Many of her shoes were outdated and worn and some of her clothes were the ones she wore many years ago, even before Tyler died. *It's time. If I'm going to start a new life for myself, then it's time to have a new wardrobe. It's exciting and frightening at the same time, but this is something I can do.* She walked into the bedroom and stood in front of her mirror. Smiling and feeling alive for the first time, she raised her voice at least ten decibels and said, "Ellie Barrett, welcome to your new world and your new life! Yippee!" She jumped on her bed, jumped back off, circled her room, singing, humming, and twirling like a six-year-old ballerina.

All evening and even this morning, thoughts of Steven were racing through her mind when her doorbell rang. Rushing to the door and flinging it open, she saw Annie with a huge grin on her face. They hugged, exchanged conversation, and then hurriedly ran to Annie's car to begin their day of shopping.

Annie was asking a million questions about Steven and was so anxious to meet him. They talked continuously with Ellie telling her all she knew to tell. She decided to save the snake incident until Mark was with them. She did give the descriptive details of Steven's physical appearance and she giggled at her own words of his sexy tanned legs and his gorgeous smile and blinding white teeth. She and Annie were both laughing and fanning themselves as they both blushed.

First stop was "Glitzy." It was a unique boutique and Ellie had always thought of going there but never had until now. As they entered the store, Ellie caught a glimpse of shimmering dresses and lots of bling. They began going through racks of dresses, but Ellie just couldn't seem to find anything that really took her breath away. If she tried on any of these dresses, she felt as if she would look like a neon sign with a zillion blinking lights.

"Annie, I think those clothes are gorgeous, but I just don't think it's what I'm looking for. Actually, I don't even know what I'm looking for, but I will know when I see it. It will stand out among all the others and scream, "Steven Monroe."' Laughing all the way to the car, they agreed that she possibly needed something a bit more reserved.

After visiting three more dress shops, they decided to take a break and have lunch. A quick salad and sandwich at the local deli gave them the renewed energy they needed for the next spree of dress shops. Their leisurely lunch gave them time to "girl talk" and share secrets and desires. Ellie loved these times she had with her daughter and wished they could do this more often, but she also was aware of Annie's own personal life and friends that occupied her time. She also knew that Annie would gladly spend time with her when either of them felt the need to share in that special bond that had formed through the years. Yes, Ellie Barrett was a very blessed woman with two extraordinary children. If only Tyler was here to see what the two of them had produced. He would be so proud.

With tiring feet and weary from looking at so many dresses, they stopped at one last dress shop for the day. While Annie browsed through the store, Ellie found a rack of dresses. As she looked at each dress and held each one up to her petite body, nothing seemed to be "the one." Frustrated and tired, she turned to Annie and was about to tell her she was ready to go when she noticed that Annie was grinning and holding up the dress that made Ellie stop in her tracks. That was it – the dress she had been searching for. She began to laugh as she told Annie, "This is the 'Little Black Dress' that every woman should have in her closet." She took the dress from Annie, held it up and gazed at it. It was perfect. Almost flying into the dressing room, she began to remove her clothes and was ready to slip into this wonder of wonders! The hemline stopped just above the knees, and it was a perfect fit all over. The lines of the dress accented her tiny waist, and it was cut low enough in the neckline to be modest but to also show off her tan and her "perky bosom." The neckline in the back of the dress scooped low and revealed her smooth and tanned skin. She was ecstatic when she saw herself in the full-length mirror. "Oh, my goodness, Annie, you have got to see this. It's the perfect dress."

When Ellie walked out of the dressing room, Annie slapped her hands over her mouth and her eyes grew large. "Mom, you are gorgeous, and that dress is absolutely perfect. Steven Monroe is going to flip out when he sees you!" They both began to giggle and laugh as they hugged.

When they reached the clerk and were ready to purchase the dress, Ellie reached in her purse for her credit card, but Annie had already retrieved her card from her purse, and she gave it to the clerk. "Mom, this is my gift to you to say how proud I am that you are finally beginning a new chapter in your life. This is a pleasure for me to do this for you." Ellie just stood there with tears in her eyes and marveled again at this wonderful daughter that God had given to her.

"Now," said Annie, "Let's go shopping for those perfect shoes!" And off they went with Ellie totally forgetting about her aching feet and tired back.

The shopping spree had ended, and Ellie was at home. As she prepared a cup of hot cider, she spread her beautiful new dress and shoes across the sofa and stared at it. Just as quickly, she glanced at Tyler's picture on the mantel. Feeling a little guilty, she walked to the mantel, took his picture, and held it close to her heart. She began to relay all the events of the day to him and then she hesitantly told him about Steven Monroe. She held the picture tightly and felt as if it would burn a hole in her chest – a hole that was about to be filled with guilt and shame and uncertainty. She had not felt this way before, but she had certainly not entertained the thought of having a date with anyone else either. Her mind raced with thoughts about the upcoming date, and she wondered if Tyler would really object or if he would be in favor of her beginning a new life. Suddenly, the beauty of the dress and shoes seemed to fade. Was she making a mistake?

She put Tyler's picture back in its usual place and she slowly walked to the sofa. With her cup of hot cider in her chilled hands, she sat down and before she knew what had happened, she began to cry, but she didn't understand why. She had not cried in quite a while and now she was letting the tears cleanse her soul.

Ellie wrapped herself in her favorite sofa blanket, curled up, and her cheeks still wet with tears, she closed her eyes and said, "God, if this is the right thing to do, please show me." Then sleep overtook her trembling and confused body.

God has His own special way of confirming the things in our lives that He's trying to show us, and Ellie was no exception. As she napped peacefully, she heard the doorbell, but it sounded so far in the distance. Perhaps she was dreaming, but it kept ringing. She realized it was not a dream and with a not-so-clear mind, she got up, walked to the door, and opened it. A young man stood there with a long narrow box tied with a large red bow. She looked around and saw the van parked in her driveway and saw the writing on it indicating it was from the local florist.

She nodded and motioned for him to wait while she ran to get some money for a tip for him, which he refused. He told her that the sender had already taken care of that, and then he returned to his van.

Ellie held the box in her arms and her heart began to pound in her chest. She already knew it was flowers, but she wasn't sure who would be sending them. Perhaps Annie sent them as a little "encouragement gift" for her. She slowly walked to the kitchen island, carefully put the box down, and saw the card attached to the ribbon. With trembling and excited hands, she opened the envelope and read the card. *"Ellie, God has truly blessed us with a special friendship. The outcome is in His hands. 'Til Friday night….Steven"*

With renewed energy and excitement, Ellie immediately removed the beautiful yellow roses, and rushed to the kitchen to get the perfect vase for the perfect bouquet. Steven Monroe was an absolute miracle in her life.

Seven

The next few days seemed to fly by as Ellie made her "to do" list and accomplished every item on her list. The house was spotless, and she had made one of her special home-made cheesecakes with cherry topping. She was hoping that after their dinner date, he would accept her offer of coffee and dessert.

Today is the day! She had been anticipating this time with some uncertainty but also with a school-girl excitement. Annie had already called her three times to see how she was and if she needed any help with her dress or with some mother-daughter conversation and encouragement. Ellie assured her that she would be fine and that she would call her the next day after her evening out with Steven.

Filling her bathtub with warm water and bath salts, she lit two candles and slipped into the water in slow motion. The warmth was soothing and relaxing as she let it rise to her neck. She let her mind wander as she enjoyed the scent of the candles as her supple body stretched out under the water.

She didn't know how long she had been relaxing in the tub until she realized the water was beginning to cool, and it was time to end this euphoric bath and begin the next step – getting dressed. She took the little black dress from the closet and gently laid it across the bed, staring at its beauty. Next, she took the new black sling heels with the tiny rhinestone bows and put them next to the dress. It was perfect!

With her dress slipping over her slender body and her shoes donning her dainty feet, she realized she was dressed for her date – well, almost. She had not given any thought to the jewelry. She had a conversation with herself in front of the mirror. "Ellie Barrett, what kind of jewelry goes with this beautiful dress? I have rhinestone bows on my shoes so I will need rhinestone earrings." She plundered through her jewelry chest and found the perfect earrings – not too small and not too large - just perfect to shimmer beneath her long dark hair. As she stared in the mirror, she knew something was missing. She needed something to bring attention to her lovely, tanned neck, but what? She didn't want any more rhinestones, or she'd light up like a Christmas tree. She looked in the already open drawer in her jewelry chest and saw the black box. With trembling fingers, she held the box in her hands and gently opened it. Her eyes were focused on the beautiful gold heart-shaped locket surrounded by tiny diamonds and emeralds. She read the inscription on the back and her heart felt the pangs of loss and hurt all over again. Opening it, she saw the picture of two people so deeply in love on their wedding day and every day afterwards – her sweet Tyler with his arm circling her waist as they stared into each other's eyes.

She wanted to wear the necklace tonight with the stunning black dress, but she wasn't sure if it would be appropriate. It was almost as if she was being unfaithful to Tyler. How could she wear it and be in the company of another man who had asked her out on a date. She put the locket back in its place in the box and quietly closed it. Just as quickly as she had closed it, she opened it again. *No, I intend to wear it. Tyler would want me to wear it and even if I'm with someone else on a date, he would still want me to wear it and not be so worried about everything.* Ellie's thoughts were running wild in her mind.

She removed the locket once again from the box and put it gently around her neck. It was perfect! It graced her neck and slightly dipped to her almost-showing cleavage. "Thank you, Tyler, for such a beautiful and loving gift. I wish you were here to see it." She fingered the shape of the locket and the delicate diamonds and emeralds, but her thumb caressed the engraving on the back as a confirmation of his love for her.

Glancing at the clock, she realized it was almost time for Steven to arrive. One last glance in the mirror and one last light spray of perfume, she picked up her matching purse to her shoes and happily sauntered into the den and waited for the doorbell to sound the beginning of her evening. She looked at Tyler's picture on the mantel and small chords of uncertainty rang through her body, but then she smiled, touched the locket one more time, and walked slowly to the door to answer the ringing of the doorbell. A new beginning!

Ellie didn't want to seem anxious, so she didn't rush to the door, fling it open, and stand there with "love-stricken" written all over her face. She walked slowly to the door and with chilled and shaking fingers, she opened it. If she thought she sounded like a blithering idiot when they first met, then this just takes the cake!

Seeing this gorgeous man standing in her doorway, she stammered and stuttered while trying to invite him in. He laughed and put her at ease as he told her he was extremely nervous, too.

Steven was dressed in a light blue dress shirt with French cuffs and beautiful gold cuff links with blue sapphire stones, a dark blue suit and a tie that was perfect for the outfit. His dark hair with a slight graying in the temple and light blue eyes were accentuated by the blue shirt. She had to admit – he was the epitome of perfection –

a model plucked from the runway. She couldn't help but notice his tanned hands and his neatly trimmed and manicured nails. On his right hand was a large gold college ring. The left hand that once was encircled with his wedding ring was now bare. She quickly glanced at her own hand and realized she was still wearing her wedding rings. Annie had told her a year ago that she should remove them, but it was just too difficult and felt it would dishonor Tyler by doing so. She didn't know what to do at this moment, but quickly asked Steven to excuse her and she would only be a moment.

As Steven waited patiently for her, she rushed to her bedroom and slowly and hesitantly slid the rings from the third finger of her left hand. A rush of guilt washed over her as she whispered, "Forgive me, Tyler. I love you."

Without looking back at the rings resting on the dresser, she held her head up, walked into the den, and with an alarming peace about her, she held out her hand to Steven, who gently placed it into his and they walked to the door. They stood on the porch with only the dim porch light shining on their faces as they looked at each other.

"By the way," said Steven, "you are stunning! You look absolutely amazing." Ellie could feel her cheeks blushing and was glad darkness surrounded them. She felt like a teenager on a first date with the star football player that every girl wanted to date.

"Thank you, Steven. I was thinking the same thing about you. You always appear so "put together." There is never a hair out of place, or you are never in faded, torn jeans and a tee shirt with dirt on it – unlike me. Oh, my goodness, I think you've seen me at my worst while working in my flowers. But you are the picture of perfection!"

Ellie almost choked on those words and wondered what in the world made her say such a thing. It was way too forward. Again, she blushed at her own remarks.

Steven thanked her and laughed as he put her mind at ease while assuring her that he had plenty of faded and torn jeans and lots of tee shirts that he wore while working in the yard or around the house. She secretly wished she could see him in tight jeans and his tanned muscled arms. She thought to herself, *Stop it, Ellie, this is so wrong – these thoughts and these feelings.* She was so glad that Steven couldn't read her mind or see her facial expression.

In the driveway sat his red sports car. It had been washed and waxed and properly detailed in every way. Thank goodness, the top was up. Ellie had spent time and effort in making sure her hair was in place and a convertible with the top down would have completely destroyed her "do." She couldn't help but think that Steven had already thought of something like that. He was such a considerate and accommodating man. She liked that. *Tyler would love this car,* she thought. As he gently helped her in the car, her mind went wild and in so many different directions. She had to exert all her energy to make herself stop thinking and to start reacting to Steven. She wasn't sure how this evening would go, but she was willing to at least be relaxed and open to conversation. Ellie Barrett was never at a loss for words – until now! Steven must have sensed her nervousness and he began the conversation as they drove to this magnificent restaurant that Ellie had heard so much about. She wasn't very fluent in French although she did take some courses in college, but that was so long ago. Perhaps Steven would understand her hesitancy in trying to order and would help her understand the menu.

They drove along well-lit streets and passed people who were enjoying their night out sitting at tiny bistro tables. Steven kept the conversation alive and as he talked about all sorts of subjects, Ellie began to feel more and more relaxed and joined in the conversation. She was surprised just how much at ease she felt with Steven and especially sitting so close to each other in this tiny sports car. The night was electric!

As Steven drove the car to the front of the restaurant, the Valet attendant was quickly at the side and opened the door for Ellie. By the time he had opened it, Steven was by her side with an outstretched hand waiting for her to softly put her hand in his. *This must be how the other half lives,* thought Ellie. She had never been to such an exquisite restaurant, not even with Tyler.

The attendant drove Steven's car away to be parked as he and Ellie made their way into the beginning of a new era for Ellie as well as into a gorgeous restaurant. French music was softly playing in the background and the aroma of food filled the air. She heard Steven say, "Reservations for Steven Monroe." She stood in wonderment at all she saw - the tiny lights twinkling along the railings and in the trees along the beautiful deck which had small tables with white linen tablecloths, crystal glasses and shiny exquisite silverware. In the middle of each table was a lovely white candle in a silver holder wrapped in greenery and baby's breath. The entire setting was mind-boggling to Ellie.

Steven put his hand at the small of her back as they followed the waiter to their table on the deck. There was another couple at the far end of the deck, so they had plenty of privacy to talk and get to know each other in a more intimate way - not working in the flower garden, killing make-believe snakes, or at church surrounded by the "Women-Seeking-Husbands" mob. This was going to be a night to remember, and Steven Monroe was going to make sure Ellie Barrett knew he existed and was there to see exactly where this friendship would lead.

Uh, oh! The menu! It was carefully placed before them, and Ellie knew she was in trouble. It was definitely in French, and there were no prices. Steven sensed her bewilderment and began to laugh quietly. He instructed her to turn two pages, and everything would be in English. She couldn't help but laugh, and also relaxed a bit more. However, Steven had another idea which thrilled her. He asked if she would like for him to order for both of them and surprise her, to which she nodded excitedly.

She had no idea what he was ordering because he was speaking fluent French and it sounded so romantic with the accent and the "roll" of the tongue on certain words. He was amazing!

They made small talk, chatting about their children, places they had traveled or lived, their likes and dislikes in food, and so many other things.

They were first served a small bowl of Crème DuBarry – a soup that she had never heard of, much less tasted. The aroma filled her nostrils, and she made sounds of delight to Steven's ears. When they completed the soup, the waiter brought their freshly made salad topped with items that she did not recognize. She couldn't help but smile at the thoughts of her salads at home with croutons out of the bag, a few extras of whatever she had in the refrigerator. But this salad smacked of careful thought and creation. She had no idea what the dressing was, but she knew on her next trip to the grocery store, she was going to try to find it. However, she also knew this was most likely a homemade dressing, and probably their specialty, and only Chef Francoise knew the ingredients.

After a few refills of their French coffee, and lots of conversation, their dinner arrived. Although Ellie didn't know what she was about to indulge in, she was anxious to try something new, which turned out to be absolutely delicious. Still a bit unsure of all the ingredients, she recognized the chicken and detected some very unusual spices. Everything was strategically placed on her lovely China plate – the chicken breast on a bed of French wild rice and covered in a sauce that Ellie had never tasted before but found it to be amazingly delicious. Steven had ordered the same and they commented on what was making the dish so explosively delicious. Ellie didn't realize how comfortable she felt and at peace with all the intermingling thoughts and fears she had been experiencing before this beautiful night took place.

They sat, talked, smiled at each other, and laughed often. Sensing the waiter had been waiting for their dinner to settle, he approached the table with two plates of Raspberry Clafoutis, which was explained to them as a baked pie cooked with fresh raspberries. The taste was heavenly as the custard and raspberries melted in her mouth. Another cup of coffee and she knew she would explode. She had never eaten so much food at one meal and everything that was served to her was beyond wonderful.

As the conversation continued and their dessert had finally settled in their already filled stomachs, the waiter approached the table with a small basket. Certainly, there couldn't be any more food for them, but there in the small silver basket with the white linen napkin and bathed in powdered sugar were six Chouquettes – French pastry sugar puffs. They looked at each other, threw back their heads and laughed until others were staring at them. Where in the world would they put these pastry puffs? Their stomachs couldn't hold another bite of food. Ellie suggested she would put three of them in her purse and he could stuff the other three in his coat pocket, and they could have them later. Laughing and giggling, they decided to just ask for a small to-go box.

When Steven was given the bill for dinner, he conversed in French to the waiter and Ellie wished she knew what he was saying. The waiter glanced at Ellie, gave Steven a "thumbs-up" and smiled. Ellie was completely in the dark, although she had an idea that there had to be a compliment in that French lingo.

Before leaving the restaurant, Steven led Ellie down a beautiful garden path lined with twinkling white lights and gorgeous flowers. The scent of the flowers filled the night air. They could still hear the faint sound of the French music from the restaurant. *Could this night be more perfect?* thought Ellie. Steven took her tiny hand in his as they strolled along the brick walkway with romantic French music filling the air. Sensing she might be a little chilled from the night air, Steven removed his coat and placed it around her delicate and smooth shoulders. She could smell his cologne on the coat and was almost mesmerized by it and by him. If only her children could see her now!

Steven and Ellie walked arm in arm back to the restaurant and Steven called for his car, which the Valet attendant promptly drove to the door. He tipped him and helped Ellie into the car. As they drove home, they continued to talk and laugh and share stories from their past with each other.

Pulling into Ellie's driveway, she knew this was the end of a beautiful evening and she didn't want it to end. As Steven helped her from the car and picking up the to-go box of French Chouquettes, they walked slowly to the door. It was only nine o'clock, and Ellie wasn't ready for this wonderful and exciting evening to end, so she quickly blurted out, "Steven, would you like to come in for some coffee and we can share the Chouquettes?" She couldn't believe those words came out of her mouth, but there they were! She was horrified that she had so forwardly invited him in. And she was more mortified that he had nodded and said he would love to. *Okay, Ellie Barrett, now what?* She thought. Too late to re-think this now so in the house they quickly went.

Ellie took Steven's coat and told him to make himself at home and she would make the coffee. With trembling hands and shaky knees, she walked into her kitchen which suddenly seemed to be closing in on her. She took a deep breath and began the task of brewing the coffee, getting two small glass plates and two coffee mugs, and placed them on the island. She thought if they sat at the island, it would be less intimate and more relaxed for both of them. She kept glancing at Steven who was looking at the different family pictures placed around the den and then she saw him stop in front of Tyler's picture and the flag in the shadow box. Her heart almost stopped. What was she going to say and how would she handle this whole situation while explaining her deceased husband and why she was dating, who would be blaming her for dating, and would Steven feel out of place there and leave? So many thoughts were flying through her mind, but Steven immediately took charge of the situation and began the conversation.

"Ellie, your husband was a very handsome man and I'm sure he served our country well. I'm very thankful for his service, and if my presence here makes you uncomfortable, tell me and I will leave."

Stopped dead in her tracks, Ellie looked at Tyler and then at Steven. "You are fine, Steven. Everything is fine. Tyler has been gone for five years and I know in my heart he would want me to begin a new life. Does having his picture before you make you uncomfortable?"

"Not at all, Ellie. He was part of your life for many years, and he deserves a rightful place exactly where you have his picture and flag. He was a very blessed man to have had so many years with you, and I'm sure you still miss him."

The magical evening they had spent together now seemed marred by memories and for the first time in a long time, Ellie was speechless as she looked at Steven and wondered if Tyler's picture had somehow sent a message straight to Ellie's heart. Was she doing the right thing, or should she be ashamed of herself for going out with another man? She tried to make small talk, but it all sounded so hollow. Sensing her emotional state, he immediately walked into the kitchen, poured a cup of coffee for her and guided her to the sofa. He then poured a cup for himself and joined her, leaving enough space between them so she would not feel uncomfortable.

"Steven, forgive me. I don't know what's wrong with me. This has been an amazing evening with you and now I feel as if I've done something wrong and been caught – sort of like being in high school and being called to the principal's office." She saw the big grin stretch across his gorgeous face and she felt the emotional strain begin to subside. They both smiled and began to laugh. That's all it took – just a simple laugh from Steven and she felt a million times better. "And, Steven, thank you for the beautiful yellow roses. It was so thoughtful of you, and I agree with the note you wrote. It's all in God's hands."

She kicked off her heels and stretched her shapely and tanned legs until her feet rested on the coffee table in front of them. Steven loosened his tie. They sat in silence for a few minutes. He reached for her hand and could feel the tension return to her body.

"It's okay, Ellie, I'm just holding your hand, you can relax. Would you like to watch a movie or a ballgame?"

"I'm not going to ruin this perfect evening and bring it to a close by watching a ballgame! How about a Hallmark movie?" Then they both laughed until their sides hurt. "Just kidding!" Ellie sputtered.

The conversation turned to the subject of their children. Ellie wanted to know everything about not only Steven, but about Abby, his daughter, and even his deceased wife. In turn, Steven wanted to know about Mark and Annie. There was so much to learn about each other, but Ellie knew there was plenty of time for personal information.

The rest of the evening was spent laughing, talking, watching a little TV, eating the Chouquettes they brought home from the restaurant, and drinking coffee. Neither of them knew or cared about the time until Ellie tried to squelch a little yawn. They both looked at their watches and simultaneously yelled, "Oh, no, look at the time!" They had enjoyed each other's company and had not even given the time a thought. It was 2 a.m.

Steven stood and began to get his coat and Ellie helped him put it on. At that very moment, something happened. Their hands met and Steven pulled Ellie to his chest. She could hear the pounding of his heart, not the soft relaxed thump, thump, but the sound of a slamming hammer. She knew he was nervous, and she also sensed that he was going to kiss her. She wanted him to, but she didn't want him to. Oh, she was so confused.

Ellie gazed upwards into his beautiful blue eyes and her gaze then went to his luscious lips, full and smooth and so very tempting. She heard a loud thumping in her ears and realized it was her own heartbeat she was hearing. As Steven lowered his head towards her face, she raised her head as their lips met.

Had she just died? Everything seemed to swirl, and her legs felt limp. What was happening to her? Was it something she ate? She didn't remember ever feeling like this before and she wasn't sure if she was elated by it or frightened by it.

Steven held her close, kissed the top of her head, and pulled away. He was walking towards the door and glanced back at Ellie. She stood there like a sagging Raggedy Ann doll – arms hanging to her side, wobbly legs, and a fixed look on her face. She knew she had to walk to the door with Steven, but she wasn't sure she could take a step. He called her name softly, "Ellie."

It must have been God who nudged her to go to the door with Steven. She managed to regain some sort of composure and met him at the door. He took her hands in his and bent down once more and kissed her on the cheek.

"May I call you tomorrow, Ellie?" She nodded and then expressed her sincere thanks for a wonderful evening. He smiled and she knew without a single doubt that he felt the same.

As she closed the door, she leaned against it and smiled, touching her lips where Steven had so perfectly placed his. This was a night she would always remember even if she never saw him again; but she knew in her heart that she and Steven would be together again.

Ellie tossed and turned for the rest of the night and kept thinking about Steven and their time together; the restaurant, the music, twinkling lights, exquisite food, and their laughter and so much more. She also felt that Tyler would approve of Steven Monroe. Finally, in a fit of restlessness, she drifted off to sleep, hugging Tyler's pillow but thinking of someone else for the first time in five years.

Eight

Ellie was tangled in her covers and the ringing in her ears was infuriating, waking her from her much-needed sleep. She turned towards the nightstand and realized it was her phone ringing. She fumbled around until she found her phone and with a groggy, raspy voice, said, "Hello." She glanced at the clock and sat straight up in bed. It was already 11 a.m. She never, ever slept this late. And then she heard the voice on the other end of the phone.

"Mom, tell me all about it. I was hoping you'd call but since you didn't, I decided I'd call you and let you fill me in on your date with Steven." Ellie pictured Annie pacing in her office, grinning from ear to ear, flipping her hair and wanting all the details. "Well, are you going to tell me? No, I have a better idea, Mom. Let's meet for lunch since it's almost lunchtime and you can tell me. I want details, Mom, D-E-T-A-I-L-S!!"

Ellie agreed that they'd meet at the local bistro downtown. She hurriedly took a shower and dressed. Already nervous about meeting and telling her daughter, she began to tremble as she applied makeup and styled her hair. Thoughts ran through her mind, *How much should I tell her? If she knew he kissed me, would she be upset and feel as if I had betrayed her dad?*

Dressed, and a bit nervous, Ellie drove to the local bistro to meet her daughter. She had a knot in her stomach the size of Texas, but she knew this was a meeting that had to take place. She didn't know if she was happy or sad that Mark wouldn't be there. He had been so protective of her since Tyler died and although she knew he wanted her to be happy, it still sent her nervous system skyrocketing. Her children were her top priority and she never wanted them to feel as if she would abandon them for a new love and adventure.

She parked her car and slowly walked to the table outside where Annie was seated. As soon as Annie saw her, she got up from her chair and raced to Ellie and embraced her. "Please, Mom, sit down and start from the beginning. I want to hear it all." She was grinning from ear to ear. She was such a romantic at heart! Ellie knew this would be a very long lunch break, but she wasn't sure where to begin or how much to tell.

They each placed their order and sipped iced tea while waiting for their lunch to arrive. Ellie cleared her throat and gave a nervous giggle as she began to tell her daughter about the awesome man and divine evening they had together. Neither of them noticed that their lunch was in front of them.

When Ellie thought of the moment Steven kissed her, she wasn't sure if she should tell her daughter all the details or perhaps save it for a later time. Just thinking of it made her heart skip a beat or two and she felt her face begin to blush. That's when Annie practically yelled out loud, "Mom, I knew it – he kissed you! He did, didn't he? Mom, tell me everything and don't leave out one single detail."

Ellie felt her face grow hotter as she imagined every person sitting at their tables now knowing about her date with Steven and that he kissed her. She knew it was no use trying to hide any of it from her daughter, so she took a sip of her iced tea and looked directly into Annie's eyes.

"Yes, Annie, he did kiss me – and it was wonderful!" They both giggled and Ellie knew at that moment that Annie would approve of the date, of Steven, of their relationship, and of anything else that would transpire in the future. Feeling relieved that Annie knew everything, she still had to tell Mark. That might be a totally different story with a totally different ending. For now, she would just enjoy being with her daughter and sharing things that only "girls" could and would share.

Just as they were finishing their lunch with giggles and laughter sandwiched between bites, Ellie heard a deep and friendly voice in her ear. "Hello, Ellie."

Ellie shaded her eyes with her hand and looked up into Steven's sky-blue eyes and immediately glanced at his beautiful smile. She smiled back at him and asked him to join them. She also knew this was the moment of truth – when Annie would finally meet "Mr. Wonderful."

With an extended hand, Annie introduced herself while Ellie just sat there in a euphoric fog. Steven gently took her hand and clasped it and then sat down with them. Ellie was still silent as she looked from Annie to Steven as if she was waiting for the sky to fall upon them. Finally, she spoke. "Steven, this is my daughter, Annie." Steven and Annie began to laugh as he said, "Yes, Ellie, we just introduced ourselves."

Okay, snap out of it, Ellie thought. "Steven, please have a seat."

"I am sitting, Ellie. Are you alright?" He was still smiling, and Annie was giggling.

"Yes, I'm fine. I just wasn't expecting you and it just caught me off guard, that's all. It's very nice to see you and I'm glad you and Annie have finally met. We just finished our lunch but would love to have you join us for dessert."

He stood up and said, "Thank you, Ellie, but I'm in a bit of a hurry. I saw you sitting here and wanted to stop and say hello. I didn't know I would be meeting your daughter, but I'm so glad that we had this opportunity to meet. Annie, it has been a pleasure." He shook her hand once more. What happened next almost sent Ellie into orbit. Steven bent down and kissed Ellie on the cheek, which was now turning blood red with excitement and embarrassment all mixed together. She was sure her mouth was drooling, and her chin had to be pressing against her chest.

"Ellie, may I please call you later this evening?" She nodded and managed to squeak out, "Yes, I'd like that." He smiled at both of them and walked away.

"Mom," Annie almost shouted, "he's gorgeous and polite and he's just the total package!" Ellie blushed again and was finding it difficult to form a complete coherent sentence. All she could say was, "I know!" They sat there giggling like two teenagers.

Lunch was over and Annie returned to work. She was so thrilled that she had finally met Steven and seemingly approved of him. She knew she wanted to get to know more about him, but for now, she had to make a phone call to Mark and tell him the news. She also knew that Ellie was dreading telling Mark because of his protectiveness, but that was one of his wonderful qualities – caring for and loving his mother and wanting only the best for her.

"Hello, this is Mark Barrett. How may I help you?"

"Mark, it's Annie. You are NOT going to believe what I'm about to tell you, so sit down!" Mark immediately sat down and asked her to slow down and talk to him. She was so excited and giggling and just blurted out, "Mom's got a boyfriend!" There was silence on the other end of the line. "Mark, did you hear me? Mom's got a boyfriend!"

"I heard you, Annie. Tell me what happened and don't leave out any of the details." Annie began to relate the fun she and Ellie were having at lunch when Steven appeared and then she began to tell him every tiny detail. When she got to the part where Steven kissed their mom on the cheek, she sensed Mark's immediate body language change, even through the phone. She knew the protective son mode just kicked in and wasn't sure what he would say. Quickly, Annie responded before Mark could say anything. "Mark, Mom's happy for the first time in a long, long time. She likes Steven and it is very apparent that he likes her, so please don't be so smothering. Give her room to breathe and to learn all over again how to possibly love someone else. She deserves to be happy, and Steven seems to make her extremely happy. Mark, it was so funny watching her as Steven sat at our table. She was like a squirming worm in hot ashes – she didn't know what to say or do. All she could do was blush and grin. It was so cute!"

Mark thanked his sister for calling and filling him in on the details of his mother's possible love life, but he was still skeptical and would continue to be that way until he could meet Steven face to face. When that happened, he would be able to make a judgment for himself. He truly wanted his mother to be happy, but the thought of it felt like a large lump in his throat that just wouldn't dissolve. However, for his mother's sake, he would make a genuine effort to meet and like this new "ray of sunshine" in her life.

Ellie wandered around in her yard and enjoyed her flowers. All the details of lunch and Steven bounced around in her head like a rubber ball on the pavement. She was glad Annie approved of Steven and she was also glad that the introduction was now over. Next, would be Mark. She didn't ask but she knew in her heart that as soon as Annie returned to her office, she would call her brother and tell him all about it….even the kiss! She touched her cheek where Steven had gently placed his lips and she felt a little quiver wiggle its way through her body. It wasn't the weather that caused it – it was Steven Monroe. She couldn't help but smile and giggle. She could hardly wait for him to call.

Nine

Sleepy, but wide-eyed, Ellie stared at the clock by her bed. Her mind was traveling a million miles an hour and she couldn't find a way to get off this horrendous roller coaster.

The clock gazed back at her as she read the digital numbers. One o'clock, then it was 2:30, and the night went on. She stared at the ceiling; flipping on her side, she then stared at the closet door, then there was the dresser mirror reflecting her troublesome body. What in the world was happening to her? She felt fine, only extremely restless. She thought of Tyler and was quickly jolted back to reality. It had to be the evening she spent with Steven! She began to recall every moment, every smile, every tender touch. Her heart melted like butter in a hot saucepan. Was she totally smitten with him or was she just excited about her new journey?

She crawled out of bed, walked to the den where Tyler's picture was displayed on the mantle. Tenderly, she removed it and held it close to her heart as she began to relay to him every detail of her date with Steven. She was surprised that she no longer felt any guilt or shame, but it was like talking with her best friend – and Tyler was always her best friend. She no longer questioned whether she should continue to see Steven or anyone else. Ellie felt a sense of freedom, peace, and contentment as she "talked" to Tyler. After an hour or two – she didn't really know for sure – she yawned, put his picture back in its place, and slowly, yet peacefully, walked to her bedroom, slid between the warm covers and let sleep consume her. She always felt better after talking with Tyler when he was alive, and now even in his death, she found comfort in their one-way conversations.

A beautiful new day and even after a restless night, Ellie felt refreshed and energized. Pouring her morning coffee, she curled up in her favorite chair and began to pray her usual prayer of thanksgiving for her blessings, etc. So many of the scriptures she had memorized through the years began to come to the forefront of her mind. Because of her close walk with the Lord, she knew He was nudging her as she reminded herself of God's goodness and how the Word of God always gave her direction and meaning in her life.

After basking in the light of God's presence and after her long talk with the Lord, she got up from the chair and happily started making her morning errand list. She just knew it was going to be a great day and an even better one if Steven would call her.

Suddenly, like a wave of cold crawling syrup, she was engulfed with dread, but what was she to dread? She was ecstatic with this new day, then it hit like a ton of bricks....she had to call her son. Mark was a wonderful and caring son, and she knew she didn't have to be afraid; but she also knew he was very protective of her and would not be as quick to accept Steven as Annie was. *May as well make the call and get it over with,* she thought. She picked up the phone and dialed his number.

"Mark Barrett speaking. How can I help you?" His deep voice sounded so much like Tyler and he spoke with such professionalism and confidence, even in only those eight words as he answered his phone.

"Hi, Honey! It's Mom." She could feel the perspiration forming on her hand as she held the phone. *Stop, stop, stop! You aren't a teenager, you're an adult and you're speaking with your wonderful son, so get a grip, Ellie!* These thoughts tumbled through her mind for what seemed an eternity. Then she heard her son's kind voice.

"Hi, Mom. It's so good to hear from you and now I want to hear about Steven Monroe." He wasted no time and Ellie was caught off guard a little bit, but she graciously told Mark that she was seeing Steven and they had a wonderful evening at a French restaurant. She also related that she and Annie had lunch and Annie knows all about Steven – even had the opportunity to meet him personally while she and Ellie were having lunch. She finally caught her breath after holding it for the entire beginning of her conversation. *Whew! Why am I so nervous? She thought. And whose voice am I hearing in the far distance?* At this point, Ellie realized she was hearing, "Mom, Mom, are you there? Can you hear me?" It was Mark.

"I'm here and I was wondering if you'd like to have lunch one day soon and I'll be happy to fill you in on all that's been going on with Steven – and me." Mark was quick to reply that he'd like to have lunch with her, but also suggested that perhaps it would be less "threatening" for both of them if he went to her house and they could relax without peering eyes from others who would be dining within ear range. Why didn't she think of that? *Ellie,* she thought, *you can be so dumb sometimes!* "Absolutely, Mark, I'd like that so much and we can have a long private talk. You name the day and I'll have one of your favorite meals for you." She could almost see him drooling at the thought of Mom's home-cooking. "Oh, and Mark?" She waited a brief second or two and then ended the conversation with, "I know Annie has already filled you in so don't play so dumb with your mom." Mark howled with laughter and told her he loved her and would call soon. She couldn't help but chuckle.

Wiping the perspiration off her hands onto her jeans, she was relieved that she had made the initial call. She had no doubt – she knew Mark would see the great qualities in Steven and would be incredibly accepting.

It was an unusually chilly day and Ellie was having difficulty staying focused on the things she had already planned to do for the day – just mundane things, nothing exciting. She rambled from room to room, never staying long enough to accomplish any particular task. Visions of Steven were rushing through her mind and although it excited her, it also carried a little apprehension, but she just didn't know why she was feeling this way. They had a good friendship, and they certainly were attracted to each other physically, so she couldn't imagine why she was sensing something was wrong – there seemed to be a "disconnect" and it was puzzling her.

Ellie had always told her children to feel free to come to her or their Dad with anything that bothered them so they could discuss it and come to some understanding of the bothersome situation. Today was one of those days for her, but Tyler wasn't around anymore, and she didn't want to subject her children to her feelings of uncertainty, especially since she really didn't know why she was feeling this way. *Ellie, if this concerns you and Steven, then you should talk to him,"* she thought. She immediately knew what she had to do and it needed to be taken care of right then.

Before she picked up her cell phone, she knew in her heart that this phone call needed to be bathed in prayer before she even dialed his number. Beside her sofa in her den, Ellie knelt and began to try to pray. No success! She couldn't pray! This was not like her at all; she was always praying, and she loved having close communication with her Heavenly Father. There was almost a hint of fear, but she didn't know why she was fearful. She began to search her mind and couldn't remember anything she had done to offend anyone, nor had she had harsh words with her family and friends. It seemed Satan was working overtime and she didn't like it. So once again, she turned her thoughts to God and this time the words began to flow.

"Lord, You know my heart. You know what's going on in my life and You also know why I'm feeling a bit uneasy right now, but Lord, I'm not sure I even know why. I need Your help. I need You to calm my nerves and give me peace. I'm in Your presence, Lord, and I am praising You and thanking You for my wonderful life. I think I'm uneasy, God, because of Steven Monroe. I really am fond of him, and I believe this friendship could develop into more, but I want to make sure it's what You want for both of us. I will never stop loving Tyler, but I believe there's room in my heart for Steven, too. Show me what to do. I only want what is best for all of us concerned and I have no doubt that You want what's best for us, as well."

Ellie remained on her knees for a little longer as she quietly continued to praise and thank Him. Slowly, she stood, scooted back on the sofa, and just sat there in total relaxation. Only God could do that for her, and she knew it. She whispered, "Thank You, God." She reached for her sofa blanket, pulled it around her and tucked it under her while she continued to bask in God's goodness. It seemed she was there for hours, but it was a time that she needed for herself – just Ellie and God. Sleep was slowly creeping in.

Her thoughts were saturated with Steven Monroe, and she suddenly felt no fear, no anxiety, no apprehension about their relationship. As his handsome face swirled through her mind, she saw the sweet smile and could hear the tenderness in his voice.

However, she couldn't quite understand the faint ringing sound in her mind.

"Oh, no! It's the phone!" Ellie realized her ringing phone had wiggled its way into her romantic thoughts. She rushed to the table in the foyer and hurriedly answered, not looking at the Caller I.D. to see who was on the other end of the line. It took her by surprise when she heard his voice.

"Ellie, are you alright?" I've tried calling you several times but could never reach you. Is everything okay at your house? I was beginning to worry and was going to go check on you if you had not answered this call." Ellie felt so cared for at this moment and if she could have reached through the phone lines, she would have taken his face in her hands and tenderly kissed him.

"I'm fine, Steven. I think I must have drifted off for a while and I do apologize for causing you any worry." Then she was silent. Steven was silent. Her house all of a sudden seemed to be closing in on her as her heart began to pound in her chest. Without realizing it and not fully understanding why, she said, "Steven, we need to talk. Can you come here this evening?" She could almost sense his tension as it took him a few seconds before he responded.

"Yes, Ellie, I will be glad to come over. Would you like for me to bring anything for us to eat?" The lump in his throat seemed to be getting larger. He wasn't sure he would even have an appetite. He sensed something wasn't right, but he didn't know what it could be. Their friendship had been growing and everything seemed to be fine. He had met Annie and she seemed to be accepting. Perhaps it was her son, Mark. He had not met him but he did know that Ellie had told him that Mark was very protective of her. Perhaps Mark had talked to her and convinced her it wasn't time for her to begin a new life. All sorts of thoughts raced through his mind, and they seemed to all be negative. What could Ellie possibly need to talk to him about?

"No, Steven, don't bring anything. I have some fresh coffee brewing and I made a coffee cake just in case either of us gets hungry."

Steven just didn't like the tone of her voice, so matter-of-fact, and not the bubbly, friendly sweet voice he had come to know and love. "Love?" Steven said it out loud. "Where did THAT come from? I haven't thought of loving anyone since Sara passed away." It was at that very moment that Steven Monroe realized he had deep feelings for Ellie, possibly even loved her, but he knew he wouldn't rush her into anything she wasn't ready for. However, based on her conversation and tone, he might not have to entertain the thought of love at all, much less discuss it. At this point, he just knew he was nervous about seeing her, afraid he would be pushed out of her life. Yes, they really did have a lot of things to talk about tonight. He also knew he had to do some sincere praying before he went to her house. This was going to be a very long night, but he also knew that God had it all under control. He just needed to be patient and follow His leading.

The day seemed to drag by as Ellie tried to busy herself with mundane things around the house. She wasn't sure why she was experiencing all these uneasy and negative emotions. She had truly been happy being in Steven's presence, so why, suddenly was she doubting their friendship? Her mind and emotions were all over the place and she couldn't seem to reel it all in to get some sort of control. She wasn't even sure why she told him they needed to talk. *About what?* Ellie thought. *I don't even know what to say or how to say it. I can't tell him I love him; that would be totally unacceptable. I can't tell him I don't think we should see each other anymore. Why would I do that? I love being with him. God, You have got to help me understand what all this is about. Tell me what to do and how to begin this conversation that is already so confusing in my mind. I want to do the right thing and I want You to lead me. Please, Lord. I'm depending on You.*

All these thoughts and silent prayers weighed heavily on Ellie's heart and in her mind. She would trust God with all of it. She continued with her day almost robotically. It was time to get dressed and presentable for Steven. She paced back and forth knowing it would soon be time for Steven to arrive. Just as if on cue, the doorbell rang. Her heart plummeted and her hands began to tremble and perspire as she slowly walked to the door. She felt as if she was swimming in quicksand – her feet didn't want to move. With cold and shaky hands, she opened the door.

One look at Steven and she wanted to rush into his arms and tell him how she felt, but she knew this couldn't happen – not now, maybe never. He stood in the doorway looking so gorgeous. The smile drew her attention to his beautiful teeth and luscious lips. His eyes twinkled but she could also detect a hint of sadness or uncertainty in them. She stepped aside and invited him in.

They slowly made their way to the kitchen where the coffee was brewing, and the sweet scent of coffee cake filled the kitchen. Ellie was so jittery that she almost dropped the coffee mug. She only nodded in his direction as if to be asking if he would like to have a cup of coffee. He said, "Yes, please." She already knew how he liked his coffee so the French Vanilla creamer and the sugar were at his disposal. Her mind was bouncing all over the kitchen and she quietly prayed, *God, help me know what to say and how to say it. Don't let me ruin this beautiful friendship.*

God heard and answered (like He always does). She immediately began to feel like herself again. She smiled at Steven, who by this time was probably an emotional wreck, too. The smile seemed to do the trick! He returned the smile and there were those gorgeous teeth and luscious lips again! She wasn't sure why, but suddenly a tiny giggle began deep within and began inching its way to her throat and then to her lips. The proverbial ice was broken.

With their coffee and the homemade coffee cake, they sat next to each other in the den. Ellie already had a fire blazing and the warmth soaked through her. She and Steven seemed to be at such ease with each other and all the dread and the doubts melted away. However, she had invited him to her home so they could talk and there was no getting around the topic. She felt such peace and contentment as she began the conversation.

"Steven, I must be honest with you. All day I have been having second thoughts about us and I don't know why. It's been a long time since I have been this happy and it scares me. What are we doing, Steven? Is this just a neighborly friendship or is it more? I don't know what to do with all this," she said as she motioned with her hands sliding them in the air from her head to her toes. "I need to know what you think and how you feel, and I need you to be honest with me, please! My fears, emotions, anxieties are all running wild right now. I'm scared to open myself to a new life with another man. I had so many wonderful years with Tyler and I'm afraid I'm feeling guilty and unfaithful. I want to move on with my life and see where God will lead me and what He wants to do in my life in terms of another relationship. Sometimes it is so difficult to trust completely." It seemed Ellie had said all this in one breath as she slowly gulped and grabbed a quick suction of air in her lungs.

Overwhelmed with emotion, Steven reached for her tiny hands and engulfed them in his. He felt her trembling and inched closer to her, wrapping the sofa blanket around her shoulders. He continued to gaze into her eyes. All he wanted at this moment was to hold her and kiss her until she could let the anxiety melt away. The time had come. He knew he had to tell her his true feelings and was mentally praying that God would help her be receptive.

"Ellie, I never thought I'd find anyone who would make me happy again. I had accepted that Sara's death would be the end of me, too. Look at us - I also never thought I'd have these feelings again, but you have stirred emotions in me that have been dormant for a long time. Yes, I'm a bit scared, too, but I'm also willing to trust God to show me, and us, what is right." Ellie shifted in her seat and began to feel more at ease. She continued to look into his eyes as he spoke to her and occasionally would glance at his lips which were already in a sweet and tender smile.

Steven continued, "I always said I would NEVER love again. I would NEVER marry again. I would NEVER allow myself to get involved in a relationship where my heart might be broken."

Ellie broke in, "Steven, never say never! We don't know what God has in store for either of us, but I do know that He knows what's best and He also knows how to bring it about. We just have to trust Him."

Steven slowly took her hands and raised them to his soft lips and kissed them. "Ellie Barrett, I have fallen in love with you!" He almost scared himself when he heard those words pour from his mouth.

She responded with such confidence that it almost frightened her as she said, "Steven, until this moment I wasn't sure how I truly felt, but I now know that I have fallen in love with you, too."

There were no fireworks, no loud booming or blasting sounds, just the crackling of the fire, the warmth of the room and two people who were experiencing love as if it was the first time for both of them. They sat and watched the fire glow as Ellie rested her head on Steven's chest. Each heartbeat that she heard pounded and echoed, "I love you. I love you." Total euphoric contentment.

They continued to talk, enjoying their coffee, nibbling on coffee cake, as they began to make some tentative plans for more dates. This would enable them to get to know each other better. It was getting late, and they both realized it was time to say good-night. They lingered at the door, arms wrapped tightly around each other, neither of them wanting to break this moment and neither of them wanting to leave the other. Giggling like two teenagers, they kissed, and Steven slowly opened the door and stepped outside underneath the amber glow of the porch light. One last glance at Ellie as she wiggled her fingers in a good-night motion. Yes, Steven Monroe was in love! Yes, Ellie Barrett was in love!

The sun seemed so much brighter, the clouds fluffier, and the sky was an azure blue. Nothing could mar this day, especially after the night she and Steven had spent talking and settling some very emotional issues between them. Suddenly, the thought of her son intruded her thoughts. *Oh, no! Mark!* She had not even told Mark about her date with Steven and her feelings that developed and now were made known to her and Steven. This was not going to be easy telling her protective son that she was in love with another man, other than Mark's father. She hoped and prayed he would be understanding and would accept Steven, first as a friend, and then whatever might be in their future. She couldn't put it off any longer.

She picked up her cell phone as she nervously dialed Mark's number. "Mark Barrett speaking. How may I help you?" His voice, sounding so much like Tyler's, jolted her.

"Hi, Mark. It's your mom." *Here we go,* she thought. "Mark, I'd like to meet with you when you have some time. I know you already know what this conversation is going to be about. After all, you talked with your sister, and I'm sure she filled you in. But I'd like for the two of us to have some time alone and let me tell you what's been happening in my life. Can you come for dinner tonight?"

"Mom, tell me what time and I'll be there." Ellie tried to pick up on his tone and decipher if he was aggravated, cautious, or just plain against her being with another man. She was at a total loss. She just trusted God with this situation, just like all the others.

"Let's make it 6 p.m. and I'll have something simple – maybe salad and a bowl of chili. Will that be fine with you?"

He replied, "See you at 6," and as if it was an afterthought, he said, "And Mom, don't worry about tonight. All will be fine. God's been speaking to my heart, too."

Like a quickly receding tidal wave, the anxiety left, and total relief replaced it. It was at this point that Ellie realized she had beads of perspiration on her forehead and her hands were moist. She didn't know why she had been so nervous about telling her son about Steven, except she knew how extremely protective Mark had become since Tyler's death. Sometimes she felt that she was engulfed in a cocoon and was being smothered, but at the same time, she knew Mark loved her and knew that Tyler would want him to care for her. It was now time to evolve from the cocoon to a new and extremely happy butterfly.

$$\mathcal{T}en$$

If anyone had come to Ellie's house on this particular day, they would have thought she was preparing enough chili to feed the entire neighborhood. Her nerves were running rampant as she mixed all the ingredients that she knew would make the chili the way Mark always raved about. She glanced at the salad that was now resting in a bowl the size of Texas, it seemed.

What am I thinking? Ellie thought. *It's just Mark and me dining together, and I'm already too nervous to eat. It looks like the leftovers will be traveling to Mark's house again.* She began to plunder through all her plastic bowls with matching lids so she could send him home with enough chili and salad to last the rest of the week. And even after that, she would still have enough to have Steven come by for a meal. *Steven – what a lovely thought.* Her mind suddenly jolted to a halt as she heard the den door open and heard Mark's tender voice.

"Mom, I'm here, and something smells wonderful." Ellie approached him and they hugged, but this time it seemed he just didn't want to let go. She thought possibly it was a bit of fear on his part of gradually letting her go so she could enjoy a life with another man. He knew it was his protective mode kicking in and he also knew he had to realize his Mom needed to move on with her life, even if it meant being with another man. He trusted her judgment and as always, he trusted God to help her make the right decisions.

After what seemed like hours of conversation and small talk, Ellie quickly removed the dishes from the table and as Mark stirred the dwindling fire, she was becoming nervous as to how to approach the subject of Steven. Sensing her nervousness, he sat in Tyler's favorite recliner, watched his mother in the kitchen, and then asked her to come and sit down so they could have the talk that she had been wanting to have for a long time.

Ellie sat on the sofa, stared at roaring fire and took a deep breath, but before she could exhale, Mark spoke up.

"Now, tell me about this wonderful man you have been hiding from me." He laughed as he said it, but she sensed his anxiousness. "Start from the beginning and as Annie would say, 'Don't leave anything out.' That broke the ice between them, and Ellie curled up, covered her legs with the sofa blanket, and smiled at her son. She began to relate the entire saga from the beginning until the present time. He listened intently, laughed a few times at her stories, but never took his eyes off her glowing countenance. He knew in his heart that she was excited about this new journey, and she was even more excited that Steven had the starring role in it.

Ellie and Mark talked for hours as he questioned her about all sorts of things, just to make sure she wasn't just suffering from "puppy love" as he and his sister had done so many times in the past. Annie was sure her twelve-year-old friend was the love of her life and that one day they would marry. Mark, equally as taken with his high school sweetheart, knew beyond a shadow of a doubt that he was in love with the most popular girl in the entire high school. He couldn't help but smile when those thoughts ran through his mind. He wanted only the best for his mother and he had to be absolutely sure that Steven Monroe was everything she had said he was.

Realizing time had slipped away so quickly, Mark rose from the recliner and gazed at his mother. He walked across the room to her, put his arms around her and gave her a kiss on the cheek, "I love you, Mom."

Ellie's heart pounded as she waited to hear the "verdict." She wondered if Mark was going to approve and if he would be willing to meet Steven. He sensed her nervousness as he said, "Mom, Steven sounds like a wonderful man and since I haven't met him yet, I can't give my full opinion of what he's like with you. Why don't you plan a date for all of us to go out to dinner so I can gain a better understanding of all of this? Call Annie and after it's set up, let me know. I look forward to meeting the man who has stolen my mother's heart." He smiled and Ellie knew it was going to be alright.

A brainstorm – that's what it was! Ellie thought how nice it would be to meet Steven's daughter, Abby, again. She met her when they moved into the neighborhood, and she had mistakenly thought Abby was Steven's young wife. This time, she would have her right mind intact, and it would be a pleasant, and hopefully, a productive evening.

Abby was a pediatrician in a town close by and occasionally she would also fill in at the hospital when needed. She knew Abby carried a heavy schedule but decided to call Steven and ask him if he would invite Abby to come to dinner. Mark wanted to meet him and why not throw in the rest of the "pack." She chuckled to herself when she thought of it that way. Her thoughts were, *Let's go on and meet the whole crowd and get all this uncertainty over with.*

Ellie made the call and Steven was delighted to know she wanted to include Abby. Everybody meeting everybody at one time - just the thought made Ellie's stomach churn like a washing machine – like wet clothes flopping and tumbling in a dryer. She was a mess! Steven assured her everything would be fine. He would call Abby and make sure her schedule would allow her to go to dinner with them.

Abby squealed with delight that her father had met someone, and he wanted her to meet Ellie and her grown children. The plans were set and Steven called Ellie to assure her that Abby was very excited about meeting them. Finally, the plans were in motion.

After many conversations back and forth, Ellie and Steven decided on a restaurant and a date and time. All three children were informed, and it would soon be the day that held a smorgasbord of emotions. Would their three adult children be accepting of each other? Did they have anything in common with each other? Most importantly, would they all be accepting of Ellie and Steven's relationship? Just thinking about it made Ellie's insides begin to shrivel up like a raisin on a hot pavement. She had to stop worrying and start trusting God with all of this.

The day arrived and Ellie was second-guessing her plan. *What am I doing? My decision- making skills are about as good as a squirrel that's crossing the street! Is all this really happening and am I absolutely sure of what I'm doing and what's about to take place? Sometimes I feel like I'm so dumb, I could throw myself on the floor and miss! Lord, please calm me down and assure me that all this is going to be fine. Right now, I feel like a tea kettle without enough steam to make it whistle. I need Your help, first of all to calm my nerves and second, to give me peace in my heart and mind that You are in control of everything in my life. I have trusted You for many years, and I trust You now. Help me make the right decisions about so many things.*

Steven and Ellie rode together and Abby, Mark, and Annie had planned to meet them at the restaurant. Steven sensed her nervousness and gently placed his hand on hers as he drove. Reassuring her, she began to relax and could feel each muscle begin to slowly find its natural place and resume its natural work. She was so thankful for Steven and his calmness in every seemingly impossible situation – at least it seemed like an impossible situation to Ellie. Just his presence had a calming effect on her. She whispered a prayer of thanksgiving to God for allowing her to find another man who was equally as kind and gentle as her Tyler had been.

Along the drive, which seemed to Ellie to take hours, she and Steven talked, laughed, and were anxious to see the children's reaction to each other and to this newly formed couple who seemed to be so much in love.

"This is going to be a very interesting evening and although I'm a bit nervous, I think it will all turn out fine. Our children are adults, have their own lives now, and I just know in my heart that they will be thrilled when they see first-hand how very much we care about each other." Ellie couldn't believe she was actually saying all this, but it came from her heart. The best part was that Steven smiled and agreed whole-heartedly.

The lights of the restaurant were now in view and both of them were beginning to scan the parking lot trying to locate the children's cars. So far, nothing. Steven parked the car, took a deep breath, gave a quick gorgeous smile and a squeeze to Ellie's hand. He was at her door, opening it and gently wrapped his strong hand around hers. It felt cold to his touch, but he understood the underlying emotion. They walked in, still holding hands, as he gave his name for the reservations he had made and explained that others would be joining them.

Walking past couples who were either enjoying their meals or couples who were simply staring at each other with "I'm in love" etched on their faces. It made them smile. The restaurant was elegant and as the waiter led them to a separate room, Ellie was impressed at Steven's plan for privacy for all of them.

Although Ellie was ecstatically comfortable with Steven, she began to feel the room closing in. It felt like the size of a shoebox and her nerves began to kick in and dance around like a bat with a radar malfunction. *Ellie, calm yourself right now. This is going to be a perfectly delightful evening and you have nothing to worry about. God's got this.* These thoughts kept coming to her mind and she slowly could feel her body relax. Just another little example of how God slips in those little blessings from time to time.

Shortly after being seated, Mark and Annie walked in. Steven stood and shook Mark's hand and greeted Annie. Ellie watched intently as they exchanged greetings and then sat down. Steven kept looking at his watch, wondering where Abby was. He explained that she was a pediatrician and sometimes her profession called for later hours. Just as he was telling them this, she walked in.

And here we go!

Beautiful long blonde hair, long legs, shapely body and a smile just like her Dad's. She wore a turquoise dress that accentuated every curve. When she approached the table, Mark and Steven both stood as Steven introduced Abby to everyone. Ellie glanced at Mark who seemed to be drooling, his eyes fixed on Abby. Ellie couldn't help but giggle inside. She knew that look and although she wasn't quite expecting it from Mark, she was pleasantly surprised that he liked what he saw.

With introductions out of the way, they ordered their food and made small talk while they waited. When their dinners arrived, Steven expressed his desire to say the blessing. This was just a natural occurrence at the Barrett household and evidently, it was exactly the same at the Monroe household. They all joined hands, which placed Mark next to Abby and he seemed thrilled to take part in hand holding. He probably had a little difficulty concentrating on the prayer while holding such a small, soft hand – he might be able to get used to this!

Dinner was delicious and laughter and conversation filled the room. Ellie and Steven watched as their children seemed to "click" in their personalities and find so much in common with each other. While watching, Ellie couldn't help but keep an eye on Mark. She knew her son well, and as she watched, she saw so many of Tyler's mannerisms. He had the same laugh as Tyler and certain hand movements were identical. She knew Tyler would be happy to see Mark easing up a bit on his worry about Ellie and would now begin to take an interest in someone his own age. A wave of relief swept over her. She couldn't stop grinning and as she glanced at Steven, who was watching her, she noticed he was happy and seemed content with the way things were falling into place among all of them.

Annie and Abby exchanged phone numbers and made a tentative date to go shopping and have lunch. Mark, looking a bit forlorn, asked if Abby would like to take in a movie sometime. She happily accepted as they exchanged phone numbers. Elation was written all over his face.

The time had come – Steven began the conversation by asking if any of them had any questions or concerns about him dating Ellie. No one had questions. They all agreed it was fantastic and they wished them well. Ellie then asked the same questions and the three shook their heads and verbally said no.

Ellie leaned into Steven and said, "Well, that was easy enough." They all laughed as they continued their conversations with each other. After coffee and dessert and more coffee, Abby was the first to excuse herself, explaining she had an early appointment with a set of 3-year-old twins the first thing the next morning. It would take all her energy just to deal with them. Mark and Steven stood as she got up from her chair. Good-byes were spoken and another round of acceptance expressed. Mark asked if he could walk her to her car. She smiled her gorgeous smile and slid her arm through the crook of his and they left. Annie rolled her eyes at her mother and started giggling. Her mother knew exactly what she was thinking. Steven knew, too.

When Mark returned to their table, he shook Steven's hand, kissed his mother on the cheek, nudged his sister on the arm (something they had done since childhood) and told them how much he had enjoyed the evening and that he trusted God to do what was best for everyone. There was a twinkle in his eye that told Ellie he already knew what God was going to do.

Annie gave her mother a huge hug and a gentle kiss on the cheek, then turned to Steven and asked, "May I hug you?" He stretched out his arms to receive Annie and gave her a big bear hug and thanked her for being close to Ellie and enjoying their time as mother and daughter. Annie left and their small room seemed so quiet. As if the air had been let out of a balloon, they both gave a huge sigh and plopped down in their chairs. The night had been a huge success. It was like a jigsaw puzzle and all the pieces were there and fit together perfectly to create a magnificently finished picture.

Ellie knew in her heart that absolutely nothing could make this night any more perfect than it already was and as she looked at Steven, the door to her heart swung wide open and she let him in. This was a new beginning for Ellie Barrett and she was willing to walk down this path of love, knowing it possibly held uncertainties, but she also knew that together, she and Steven could make this beautiful relationship become a permanent one.

Nothing could mar this wonderful evening for the Barretts or the Monroes – absolutely nothing!

Eleven

"Hello." Steven's voice was ragged and raspy from the early morning hour and his eyes quickly glanced at the clock beside the bed. Four a.m. and who on earth would be calling at this ungodly hour? He held the phone in his hand, but no one said anything. He kept repeating, "Hello, hello. Is anyone there? Who are you calling?" Still no response. Thinking it was a prankster or possibly a wrong number, he hung up the phone, turned back over and covered himself with the warm blanket, and was soon asleep again.

Once again, the phone rang, and Steven answered it, this time a bit more brusquely. He didn't recognize the area code and thought it might be another prankster, telemarketer, or another wrong number.

"Hello, this is Steven Monroe. Who's calling, please?" After a brief moment, a woman's voice spoke softly. He immediately recognized it and broke out in a cold sweat.

"Hi, Steven. This is Darlene and I hope I'm not calling too early." He glanced at the clock and saw a bright red glow that told him it was past time to get up. He never slept this late. It was 9:30 and he was still sleeping. It had to be because he had experienced a wonderful, but mentally and emotionally exhausting evening with

Ellie and the three children. He was completely drained when he went to bed and slept soundly as he dreamt of Ellie.

"Darlene, why are you calling me? Where are you?" He sat up in bed, ran his fingers through his hair and his mind raced like a NASCAR driver. Why on earth would she be calling him after all this time? She had been determined to have Steven in her life. She had told him she loved him and wanted a future with him. He had explicitly told her he was not interested in any other woman other than his deceased wife, but she wouldn't accept that answer. She showed up at the most inopportune times which caused him to become almost paranoid. Wherever he went, he looked around to see if she was near-by. He was dreading any encounter with her. There were times he would see her in the distance and he would backtrack his steps, or go in the opposite direction, just to avoid contact. These were miserable few months for Steven, and he didn't waste any time trying to be invisible.

"Steven, I have missed seeing you and then I heard you had moved. You have no idea how much trouble I have gone to just to try to find you, and VOILA! Here you are! I'm so happy to hear your voice and I can hardly wait to see you again."

Steven's stomach began to churn. Darlene Eversby was the last person on earth he ever wanted to see, talk to, or be around. His mind whirled with all sorts of thoughts, but most of all, Ellie came to his mind. Her sweet and kind smile, the way she twirled her beautiful dark hair around her finger, and her gentle touch to his face. *Ellie, oh my goodness, Ellie – what is she going to think or say when I tell her about Darlene? I should have told her in the beginning, but I never thought it even deserved wasting my breath on a conversation about her. Oh, my sweet Ellie, how am I going to make this right?*

"Darlene, you should have never contacted me. I told you a long time ago that there was nothing between us and there never would be, but you kept pursuing the idea that you could make me love you. I don't love you and never have. If I ever gave you the idea that there was anything at all between us, I do apologize – again! Please don't call me again and don't show up any place where you think I might be. Please, Darlene, please leave me alone!" He hung up, noticing the marks of perspiration from his hand still on the phone. Steven didn't want to be rude, but he was feeling a bit uneasy about her and what she might do to interfere with his new-found love for Ellie. He knew he had to get alone with God and get his thoughts and his emotions under control.

Fearful that Darlene would call again, he turned the phone off, but what if Ellie called – he'd want to answer it. He just trusted the Lord on this one – that the phone wouldn't ring at all during his conversation with God. God heard and answered.

After a long talk with God, Steven got up from his knees and felt such relief, as if a heavy load had been lifted from his shoulders. He also knew he had to tell Ellie before Darlene found a way to get to her and fill her mind with all sorts of untruths. This was not going to be easy to do, but he loved Ellie and wanted no secrets between them. The idea of telling her about Darlene had not even crossed his mind because there was nothing to tell. She was among throngs of women who "came to his rescue" when his wife died. You know – the ones bearing casseroles, sad condolences, and offers to help in any way he needed. Darlene had been one of them, but she was like a pit bull that had a grip on his pants legs and wouldn't let go. She was determined to make him all hers. As graciously as possible, he had tried to make her understand he was grieving and not interested in another woman, no matter how good the casserole might have been.

A cup of coffee trembled in Steven's hands as he picked up the phone to call Ellie. He dialed and the sound of her sweet, happy voice seemed to make everything right.

"Good morning, Ellie. I hope you slept well, and you are ready to face another beautiful day. I wanted to hear your voice this morning and make sure I was not still dreaming. We did have a great evening last night, didn't we? All our children were there, and we all had a wonderful and relaxing time. That did all happen, didn't it?"

Ellie felt a bit confused, but laughingly reassured him that it all happened and that everything was great. Being as tuned in to Steven as she was, there seemed to be something in his voice that sounded out alarms, but she couldn't imagine what it might be.

"Steven, is everything alright? I sense something in your voice that says the opposite. Am I imagining things or is there something you need to talk to me about. I'm feeling a bit frightened right now and this is not a good feeling. Come over to the house and we'll have some coffee, and we'll talk. I sense there is definitely a subject you want to discuss. Am I right?"

"Ellie, I'll be right over. And Ellie, I love you." She practically dropped the phone! *He loves me? He just said he loves me. He's never said that before and frankly, I was hoping it would be in a more romantic setting, but I don't understand why he said it at this particular time, on the phone, and is rushing over here to talk. God, I need your help right now. Whatever is going on, I need you to keep me calm, keep my mouth shut as I listen, and then give me the words I need to say in response.*

She had hardly finished her last words to the Lord when the doorbell rang. *Wow, that was quick. Did he fly?* She opened the door and gazed at what used to be a gorgeous, tanned face and bright white teeth. His face seemed taut, and lines burrowed his forehead. And his hair? What in the world happened to the well-groomed hair? She knew something was wrong.

"Steven, please come in and let's get a cup of coffee." She knew how he liked his coffee, one teaspoon of sugar and French Vanilla flavoring. Along with the coffee, she had a Cheese Danish, already warmed. She took their coffee and Danish and walked to the table. She couldn't help but remember all the late-night chats she and Tyler had at this same table and all the conversations they had with the children over different matters. This was a table of love and it seemed it was where many solutions to problems took place. Today was no different. Here was Steven, evidently disturbed about something, and she was quietly praying that a solution would be found at this table of love and understanding.

They both sat in silence, twirling their spoons in the coffee mugs, barely nibbling at the Danish. Ellie's heart felt like it would explode. She was scared and yet, she was curious. Nothing could have happened between them since last night. It was a glorious evening together and everything went just as planned, even better, so what happened?

"Okay, Steven, obviously, something is wrong, and we need to talk about it. There is nothing you can tell me that will change my mind about anything that is going on between us. So, please, sit back and relax, and tell me from the beginning. Whatever it is, we can handle it and with God's help, it can be solved."

Steven's hand slowly reached for hers and he held her small hands in his. She could feel him trembling. He looked at her, and she thought she detected a small blur of tears. She tightly squeezed his hand and reassured him with her touch that it was going to be alright. He began to tell her about the phone call at 4 a.m. He was almost certain it was Darlene, but he then told her about the call later that morning. His heart pounded in his chest as fear crept in and told him he would lose Ellie.

"Ellie, Darlene meant nothing to me, and I really think she is to be pitied. She is so desperate to have a man in her life. She kept pursuing me. It seemed everywhere I went she was there and would always make it a point to come to me and put her arms around me and stare at me. It was a very uncomfortable feeling and although I would ask her to back away, she just continued to find me."

"Is that why you moved here" Ellie asked, "to get away from Darlene? Steven, you cannot run from situations no matter how bad they get. I believe she would have eventually moved on to someone else; however, I must say she knew perfection when she saw it and I can't blame her for tracking you down all the way to right here in my neighborhood." Ellie began to grin and then burst out in laughter as she stared at a very confused Steven.

She assured him that she was not concerned or worried at all about Darlene and she was so sorry that he even considered that there would be a problem with all of this. She reached for his hand and felt the trembling become less and less.

Rising from her chair, she walked to his side and tenderly cupped his face in her hands, looked into his eyes, and said, "Steven Monroe, on the phone you hurriedly told me you love me. Do you remember saying it?" He nodded and couldn't take his eyes off her pretty smile. Then Ellie took a deep breath, lowered her petite body so she could be eye level, and whispered, "I love you, too, Steven Monroe." Their lips met and everything was back to normal. Steven wrapped his arms around her so tightly she could hardly breathe, kissed her again, and repeated over and over how much he loved her. They both knew that whatever shenanigans Darlene might try to pull, they were both ready, and together they would conquer this battle. They had a rock-solid strong faith in God, and they trusted Him completely to help when needed.

After their conversation, they sat together on the sofa, sipped their coffee, and began to make plans for the evening. Ellie felt so content, relaxed, and totally happy – even with the thought of Darlene dangling over their heads. She wasn't worried at all – or was she?

It was settled. They discussed options, but finally decided that he was going to cook dinner for her at his home and she wouldn't have to do anything except arrive and enjoy the meal and the evening. Nothing fancy, just a night to prop up their feet, enjoy a roaring fire, and maybe watch a movie. It sounded like a perfect night and Ellie could hardly wait until the evening arrived.

She walked Steven to the door, but inconspicuously glanced around the street to see if there were any strange cars or people milling around. There was nothing. The neighborhood was quiet – for now! They stood in the doorway, Steven leaning against it and Ellie leaning into Steven. Neither of them seemed to be able to quit smiling at the other one. They tenderly kissed and he turned to go home. She stood there waving at him as he kept turning around looking at her as if she might disappear into a vapor. Oh, how she loved him, and she loved how he made her feel. Then she yelled, "Steven, please do something with your hair!" She was laughing as she closed the door.

Walking back into the den, her mind was blurred with thoughts of Steven, and she was so thankful and so blessed to have him in her life. Then it hit! She began to have a conversation with herself. *Ellie Barrett, what is happening? What just happened with Steven? What about Darlene? What about Tyler? How can I ever make this right with Tyler? Will he understand and would he really want me to move on with my life? I promised myself I would NEVER let another man in my life. I would NEVER love anyone else and I would NEVER get married again. MARRIED? Where did THAT come from? Ellie, get control right now!*

She slowly, almost ashamedly, walked into the den and there were those kind and gentle eyes staring at her from the mantle. Tyler's picture seemed to come to life as she approached the framed picture of the man she had loved for so many years. The man she had given her heart to and promised to never let anyone or anything come between them. She recalled their many conversations about his military duties and the dangerous possibilities that could happen. She remembered holding him close to her and telling him she would NEVER want another man if something should happen to him. She would NEVER fall in love and get married again. Reminding him of her deep love for him, she couldn't imagine anything like that ever taking place. She didn't want it to take place, and she intended to keep her word. Ellie could almost audibly hear Tyler's remark to her as he grinned and said, "Ellie, never say never!"

After an exhausting day filled with errands and house cleaning, Ellie had tried all day to keep her thoughts at bay, but the picture of Darlene kept entering her mind. She wondered about her looks, her age, her determined pursuit of Steven. She had heard of, and probably knew a few, women like that – those who wanted a man at any cost. She just didn't know she would ever be able to experience it firsthand, and she didn't like the uneasy feeling that kept churning in her heart, her stomach, and her spirit. What if..........

Steven had not called since he left her house this morning with the bombing news about another woman who was tracking him. Without waiting another moment, she picked up the phone and dialed his number. He didn't answer and her imagination began working overtime. She tried again and then a third time. Each time she hung up, refusing to leave a message. Almost thinking out loud, she began to speculate in her mind. *What if he's out with Darlene – what if she's at his house and that's why he didn't answer the phone – what if they are in some compromising situation – what if Steven isn't really who I think he is.* She had worked herself into a frenzy and couldn't stand it any longer. She tried calling again and still, no answer. There was nothing left to do but get dressed, parade herself to Steven's house and ring the doorbell. Her stomach turned over another time as she thought about what she would do if she found out that Darlene was at his house. How would she ever be able to handle it? Okay, it was time for prayer.

Immediately Ellie retreated to her bedroom and fell to her knees beside the bed. Seems she had been spending a lot of time in this position lately, but she had to be sure about so many things and only God had the answers. She poured out her heart to Him and asked for wisdom and understanding. She told God how she felt about Steven, that she loved him (like God didn't already know it?) On and on she went until she felt the relief she was praying for. Rising from her knees, she decided to call one more time.

"Hi Ellie. I'm so glad you called..." But before he could say another word, she burst into tears. He could hear her crying but had no idea why. "Ellie, stay right there – I'm on my way."

Steven was dumbfounded. He couldn't imagine what had happened. Then her name pounced into his mind – Darlene! Could she have possibly found Ellie and confronted her? He couldn't get to Ellie's house fast enough - for the second time this day. It seemed to him that the tables had turned and now it was Ellie who seemed troubled about something.

Ellie saw him running up the driveway and she opened the door. Tears were streaming down her face, and she couldn't stop them. Immediately Steven shut the door and wrapped his arms tightly around her and let her cry, her head resting on his shoulder. His mind was racing and wanted to approach the subject but thought it would be best if Ellie enlightened him about the tears and the reason behind them.

She took his hand and led him into the den, and they sat side by side on the sofa. Her face was red and tear-stained, and she couldn't help but let a little hiccup escape. Steven was beginning to feel fear crawling through him as he stared at her, his eyes filled with love and compassion, but also along with it was a niggling feeling that Darlene was somehow mixed and mingled throughout this process.

"Ellie, whatever this is all about, we can talk about it and resolve it." He was so sincere and wanted nothing more than to make everything right for her.

She finally caught her breath enough to begin her conversation with him. "Steven, I called you several times and you never answered your phone. You were here this morning telling me about Darlene and then when you didn't answer, my mind started going crazy. I don't like the way it made me feel and I don't like to think you were with her. I don't even know if you were with her or not, I just don't like it." She was babbling on and on.

Gently rubbing her hands, he said, "First of all, I have been home all day. I have been working in the garage, sorting out boxes and tools and I accidentally left my cell phone in the house. Why didn't you leave a message? I had planned to call you just to tell you how excited I am about our date tonight. I am so sorry you thought I was with Darlene. My sweet Ellie, there is no other woman for me except you. I told you I love you and that hasn't changed and never will."

A thought jolted her – *Oh, no, there's that word again – Never!*

Feeling her body begin to go limp, she rested her head on the back of the sofa and let out a huge sigh of relief. A weight had been lifted and she felt like she could breathe normally again. Turning her head towards Steven, she smiled and without any hesitation, said, "Steven, I love you so much." He held her in his arms, and they kissed tenderly as his hands gently rubbed her back. Ellie knew without a single doubt that this man was truly the one God had placed in her life and all the Darlenes in the world could not break the bond between them. They would fight this fight – all three of them – Ellie, Steven, and God. Darlene would not win this battle. God would!

Twelve

With the conversation about Darlene completely settled in Ellie's mind, she knew she would have no worries about this "other woman." With a burst of energy, she began to prepare for her date with Steven. She had deliberately kept the subject of Darlene just between Steven and herself and did not want her children to know. If Annie knew, there would be a million questions and ways to get this other woman out of the picture. Ellie just didn't want the hassle of all of this, and she knew there would be so much drama if Annie got involved in it. With Mark, it might take on a totally different color. He was very protective of his mother and Ellie could almost see that protective mode kick in and she had no idea how Mark would handle this. No, Ellie knew they could never know about Darlene; after all, she was just a woman from Steven's past and one he had absolutely no feelings for and never had. Maybe one day she would jokingly tell her children about Darlene, but for now, it stayed between her and Steven.

Ellie and Steven had a wonderful evening together on their date. They had made the decision to go out to dinner instead of Steven cooking for her. That would be for another night. After the morning of emotional roller coaster rides, they just needed to have a change of scenery. It was a night of being light-hearted and acting like giddy teenagers. There was pizza, music, and some folks were even dancing to the tunes they liked. Ellie noticed that she had even kicked off her shoes and had her feet folded under her like she used to do when she was a teenager. She and Steven laughed, made plans, drew hearts and little sweet sayings on their paper placemat. She had not felt like this in a very long time, even though she was always happy when the two of them were on a date or even just sitting at home by the fire watching a movie. Her heart kept whispering, *you love him, he loves you. Now what?*

Two weeks flew by, and she and Steven continued to see each other every day and/or night. From the time her eyes opened to the morning sun, she began feeling that happiness knowing she would see him again this very day. Ellie was in love!

In her "nothing can ruin my day" mood, she ran to answer her ringing phone. She knew it was going to be Steven, just like every other day.

Feeling a bit playful, she answered in a low, soft, and completely out of character voice. "Hel-l-l-o-o, handsome!" She was so certain it was Steven that she didn't even look at the Caller ID.

"Well, I've never been called handsome before, but I have been told I'm quite a beautiful woman. You must be the one Steven is so infatuated with. Before you answer me, let me assure you that Steven and I have a past together and I plan for us to have a future together, so you might want to consider backing off. Don't be fooled by his good looks or his mesmerizing charisma and think that he wants you. He has me! My name is Darlene and I'm glad I found you. Leave him alone or my next step will be to show up at your house and I'm sure you don't want to have any kind of confrontation. Good-bye." There was only the dial tone, which seemed to hum on and on. Ellie never had the chance to say a single word.

This cannot be happening, Ellie thought, *I have to call Steven and tell him. He's going to be furious, but we promised we'd be in this together and with God's help, we would get it resolved.*

Her happy day had turned to one of anxiety, possibly a bit of fear, and she felt wrapped tightly in uncertainty, but she also knew God was her refuge and strength. She had read that scripture verse so many times in her Bible and even had it underlined and highlighted. She believed it.

Walking slowly to the phone, she dialed Steven's number, and he answered on the first ring. He knew it was Ellie. "Hi, beautiful, I'm so glad you called. What's on our agenda for today?" There was silence on the other end of the line. "Ellie, are you there? Please answer me." He suddenly felt a wave of nausea rolling through his stomach. "Ellie, what's going on?"

"Steven, I'll be right there." He recognized the tone of her voice and knew it was a mixture of fear and anxiety. "Hurry, Ellie, I'll be waiting for you." Something within him told him it had to do with Darlene and at the very thought of it, his love and concern for Ellie quickly turned into anger for Darlene. He knew he had to be careful and not let Ellie sense this deep disdain he had for this woman who had suddenly crept into his and Ellie's life, but he also had to assure Ellie that Darlene was a very disturbed woman and to be careful.

The door flung open, and Steven was there with open arms and Ellie flew into them. Her heart felt as if it would pound out of her chest. She knew she and Steven were in love and she also knew they had made a vow to share everything about this horrid woman.

Walking slowly to the soft, but masculine, sofa, Ellie limply dropped onto the cushion. Steven was making a cup of hot tea for her. There was total silence while he prepared the calming lavender tea. Putting the cup on the table in front of her, he sat down, took her hands, kissed her, and asked her to tell him everything. Somehow, he already knew.

"It was her, Steven, it was her!" I thought it was you calling, and I answered in a rather provocative voice, just being funny, and it wasn't you. I am so embarrassed. I know she thought I was some sort of tainted woman answering the phone like that." She demonstrated how she answered with "Hel-l-l-o-o-o-o handsome!" He burst out laughing and she couldn't help but join in. He always made her feel so much better.

She proceeded to relay the conversation to him almost word for word. She told him she never had the opportunity to say a single word. Then, in her most serious voice, she looked at Steven and said, "Now what? What happens next and what am I supposed to do? This is a bit frightening to me, Steven. I mean, what if this crazed woman shows up at my house at whatever hour of the day or night she wants to – what do I do?"

"I'll take care of this, Ellie. You don't have to worry. I promise, I will make sure she understands how much I love you and no one will come between us. I'll take care of it."

After a few minutes of thought, Ellie told Steven that she wanted to confront Darlene with him. She didn't want him to be alone with Darlene, not because she was worried about what might happen with Darlene's twisted mind, but because she thought Darlene might get a better understanding if she saw the two of them together and would know that they could not be separated. She watched as Steven listened and wondered if he would agree to her suggestion. Finally, he agreed. Ellie's heart rate slowed back to normal, and she felt such protection as she rested in Steven's arms. She wished she didn't have to leave. She didn't want to return to her empty house. If only she could stay forever wrapped in his strong arms and feeling his tender kisses on her forehead and then her lips.

As Ellie walked to the door, he held her hand and looked deeply into her eyes. "Ellie Barrett, I am in love with you, and I find it more and more difficult to say good-bye. I wish you could stay forever." Her hand slid from his and reached for his face. With emotions boiling inside and a desire to act on those unleashed emotions, she kissed him, told him she loved him, and left. Hot salty tears ran down her cheeks and dripped from her chin as she made her way to her empty and extremely lonely house. She wasn't even sure why she was crying.

The remainder of the day, Ellie busied herself with household chores, but each time she heard a creaking board or just the rumble of the ice maker, she would jump and immediately look all around her. She knew she was just being paranoid, and she seriously needed to get some control. The only thing that kept her sane for the rest of the day was knowing that she and Steven would be going out to dinner together. Their dinner dates were always so relaxing, and they spent time talking and planning and laughing. She loved the deep sound of his laugh, so genuine and so masculine. She would concentrate on their date for the next few hours until it was time to dress for the occasion.

Right on time! Opening the door, she stepped back, almost toppling over the chair. She had expected to see six feet of gorgeous flesh, dressed to the nines, and ready for a wonderful evening. Her eyes widened and she was speechless. All she could do was stare.

"Hello, Ellie." The well-manicured hand extended towards Ellie. "I'm Darlene and I thought it would be best if I came to your house to let you know that Steven and I will be going out to dinner tonight so you may as well change into whatever you wear around your house and just plan to have dinner alone."

Ellie was dumbfounded. She couldn't speak – all vocabulary was lodged in her throat and her body was trembling. How dare this woman show up at her house and tell lies about Steven. Without further hesitation, Ellie stepped to the door, held it open and told Darlene to leave. There was almost a demonic sound to Darlene's laughter as she reached for the door and slammed it and pointed a long finger in Ellie's face. Then she grabbed Ellie's arm, twisted it behind her back and began to spew profanities in Ellie's ear. Ellie screamed in pain and just as she did, the door flew open, and Steven rushed in. Seeing the scene, he became livid. Fire flashed in his blue eyes as he approached Darlene. She immediately released Ellie's arm and rushed to Steven.

"Sit down NOW, Darlene." He hurried to Ellie, who was fighting back the tears. The two of them approached Darlene and Steven began to tell Darlene, again, that he had no interest in her and never had and never will. He continued to describe Ellie and her sweet, gentle spirit and his love for her. Darlene began to squirm in her chair but wouldn't make eye contact with either of them. It was obvious that Steven was relaying the message in such a manner that Darlene was finally comprehending it.

Standing, Darlene spoke. "This is extremely painful for me to hear and to watch the two of you together, but you have made it perfectly clear that you have no interest in me. I had only hoped if I couldn't get through to you, Steven, then perhaps I could make Ellie understand how much I love and need you. I can see I was wrong." She turned toward the door, slowly opened it and looked back to see Steven and Ellie in a tight hug, arms around each other and he was kissing the top of her head while bringing her even closer to his body.

"Good-bye, Steven. I'm very sorry. Ellie, I can see you both love each other." She closed the door quietly while Steven and Ellie (especially Ellie) held their breath until they heard the roar of the car engine about a block away from where she had hidden her car.

They looked at each other and Ellie did a little jiggy dance and Steven gave the old air pump with his fist. They knew it was over and they could get on with their lives – they hoped!

The excitement and energy Ellie had felt while waiting for Steven's arrival had now left her deflated and drained. Her emotions were all over the place and Steven sensed it. He tenderly took her in his arms and held her for as long as she felt the need to be held. She could feel his heartbeat and as it slowed its pace, she began to fully relax, still wrapped in his arms.

Finally, Ellie wiggled out of his embrace and looked deep into his eyes as if she could see into his soul. He always made her feel safe and she rested in that calming sense of pure satisfaction. Without any hesitation, she said, "Steven, I love you so much and I have no doubts about our relationship. It's pure and honest and overflowing with mutual respect. And even though I was momentarily frightened by Darlene's behavior, I know that it's me that you love, not Darlene. My heart truly aches for her. She has been so wrapped up in her desire to have you that she's lost all sense of direction in her life, and she's lost in a sea of hurt, pain, and hopelessness. Instead of condemning her, we should be praying for her. I don't fear her at all."

"That's one of the many reasons I love you, Ellie. You are always looking on the bright side of situations and you have such a heart for people – always wanting to help them and give them a sense of belonging and self-worth. You are an amazing woman, Ellie Barrett, and I am so much in love with you." He tenderly kissed her and at that very moment, Ellie knew she would one day marry Steven Monroe.

Ellie and Steven had an extremely memorable evening as they relaxed at one of their favorite restaurants – nothing fancy, but enough ambiance that they could both sense the intense feelings they were having for each other. They both enjoyed coffee with

French Vanilla flavoring and shared a large slice of fresh coconut cake. There wasn't much conversation, but they each knew what the other was thinking. The love they felt for each other was surrounding them and wrapping them in a dense fog of total euphoria. It was as if no one else was on the premises and no one else could see or sense their deep affection for each other; they were in another world of their own. Finally breaking from this state of ecstasy, Steven spoke while holding Ellie's hand close to his chest. She could feel his heart racing.

"Ellie, I love you and I have no doubts that you love me, too. My question is this – where do you want all this to go? Are you ready to take our relationship to the next level? Are you ready for the children to know exactly how we feel and that we want to move ahead with our lives together?"

She sat motionless, afraid this moment would vanish and she would never be able to recapture it. With a shaky voice, she responded with a joyous "YES" as she rushed from her side of the table to sit beside him. She threw her arms around his neck, pulled him to her and kissed him as if it might be the last time they would ever see each other. Even during her kiss, she was giggling – excited beyond words and the happiness she felt was filtering all through her body. It had been years since she had felt this way. Not since, well, not since Tyler. His name in her mind brought her back to reality. She knew Tyler would be happy for her; he never wanted her to be alone or lonely, and she knew he would approve of Steven. How had she been so fortunate to be so blessed to have been loved by Tyler and now loved by Steven? God was so good.

On their ride back home from the restaurant and with a new sense of depth to their love for each other, they were both chattering back and forth and sometimes they were talking simultaneously. They both felt the electricity between them as they talked about the future. Their children would be happy for them, they were sure of that. They discussed having dinner together with their children and letting them know of their love for each other. Both of them wondered about Mark's reaction, but Ellie felt certain that he would approve, especially seeing how happy his mother was. As for Abby and Annie, well, they would be ecstatic. Girls react that way!

Even though Steven and Ellie were in love, there was no mention of marriage and that made her wonder just a wee bit about his intentions. *To be sure, he doesn't expect us to date forever, and I know he doesn't mean for us to just date and become intimate, because that just isn't going to happen,* she thought. She pushed the thought to the back of her mind and decided to let God take care of that part of their relationship. She would just bask in the beauty of the love she and Steven felt for each other and rest in the assurance that God would either bring it all to fruition or He would provide a way for it to end peacefully and with a kindred friendship. She wasn't worried at all. She had trusted God in so many situations in her life, why shouldn't she trust Him now? All was well.

Thirteen

With an agreed-upon date, Ellie and Steven both called their children to set up a time for the five of them to get together for dinner. After talking with the children, everyone had agreed upon a date, time, and place. Now the real fits of anxiety and tiny bubbles of fear rose in Ellie. She began to play the "what if" game…. what if they got upset when possibly the subject of marriage was mentioned? What if Mark refused to accept this type of relationship for his mother? What if Abby just didn't want another woman to replace her deceased mother? What if Annie didn't want another man to replace her deceased father? So much was running through Ellie's mind, and she realized her hands were balled into fists and the vein in the side of her neck was bulging and pulsing.

"God, please calm me and reassure me that all is going to be alright with our children." Immediately, she felt herself relax, and a gentle peace began to wash over her. She knew God had heard and answered – again!

Ellie and Steven talked on the phone for hours or they were at each other's house for hours. She knew the time was getting close for the two of them to be meeting the three children. They talked about the "what ifs" and how they would answer their questions and reassure them of their love for each other. It was going to be an interesting, and possibly a very long, evening as Ellie and Steven would tell the children about their feelings and how they would love to have their blessing in this relationship.

The sun had already disappeared, and evening was making its way in the neighborhood. Ellie was sorting through some clean and folded laundry, searching for her favorite pajamas. It was still early, but with the sun setting so early, it felt as if it was already bedtime. Just as she crawled into her pj's, her phone rang. Rushing to answer it and hoping it was Steven, she curled up on the sofa, smiled, and took his call. His gentle voice echoed through the phone line, soft, calming, and sexy. Ellie was already beginning to feel the warmth soar through her body. They laughed, talked about their day, and discussed the next night with anticipation – the night they would draw their children into their personal lives and tell them what was going on. Ellie was nervous about it, but Steven seemed quite assured and confident. That was one of his many qualities that Ellie loved. They continued to talk until Ellie began to yawn. Sensing her weariness, Steven gently told her he loved her, hoped she would sleep well, and he'd call her the next morning – if he could wait that long. They both giggled as they touched the red button on their phones, disconnecting them.

The day flew by for Ellie as she did her usual household chores and prepared her mind for the evening. This was going to be extremely interesting as she anticipated the outcome. She knew she would have to leave it completely in God's hands. Every time she left impossible situations in His hands, He would always solve the problem. *Why do I doubt? He's never failed me yet and I know He won't fail me this time! Ellie, relax. God's got this one!*

Several times during the day Ellie would pause in front of the mirror and "practice" her part of the speech, and each time, she would change it. How would all this play out? She continued to gaze in the mirror at this "new" woman. She saw her reflection and admired her tiny figure – the one Tyler had always complimented her on each time he looked at her. Tyler! She knew she would never forget him. Every time she looked at her children, she saw him. Each time they would laugh, she would hear his voice. Was she doing the right thing, getting involved with Steven? Her mind flew at record speed again as she began to re-think this new relationship. She also knew in her heart that she loved Steven. *Ellie, stop right now! You've prayed and now let God work it all out. Get out of His way!* One more glance and she moved away from the mirror and made her way to the bathroom to complete her makeup routine. It would soon be time for Steven, and she wanted to greet him at the door in a display of grace and beauty. *That's funny, Ellie – grace and beauty? Sounds like a line from an old Grade C movie!*

Steven was on time and when Ellie opened the door, he stood straight and tall and said, "Ellie Barrett, I love you!" He wrapped her in his arms, like so many times before, and they stood in the doorway basking in each other's love.

The ride to the restaurant seemed to take forever, but at the same time, it seemed not long enough. They were both a bit nervous, not knowing the reaction of the children, but hand in hand, they walked in and were directed to the table where three lovely adult children sat. Ellie swallowed, gripped Steven's hand, and sat in one of the empty chairs which happened to be beside Mark. Steven sat between Abby and Ellie. Annie sat to the right of Mark. Everyone was chatting, giggling, and Ellie noticed Mark eyeing Abby. It seemed they had a secret code between them, and Ellie was dying to know what was going on with the two of them. Mark was a very private person, so Ellie didn't always know the ins and outs of his personal life, but tonight there seemed to be electricity in the air.

Was it for Mark and Abby or for Ellie and Steven? They would soon find out.

Dinner was delicious and the table talk was refreshing and entertaining. They were all chatting with each other and finishing their dessert when Annie said, "Alright," looking directly at Ellie and Steven, "we all know that this isn't just another night out for all of us. We know there is something different about tonight and we're all prepared to hear what's going on, so out with it!

Steven squeezed Ellie's hand under the table as they both swallowed, gulped, and stared at the three children. Then they looked at each other as if to say, *You go first. No, you go first.* One last glance at each other and Steven began to speak.

He told them how they met, the dates they had shared, the quiet times at home with each other, and all the funny experiences they also shared together. It seemed his part of the conversation lasted forever and then he turned to Ellie. Her hands were damp with perspiration, and she could feel it trickle down her back. She knew she shouldn't be this nervous around their children and especially with Steven there beside her. He was her comfort and rock through so much. Tonight was no different.

She called each child by name and told them that she loved them. She referred to Tyler from time to time, as a way to assure her children that he would always have a place in her heart. She shared her feelings for Steven and watched intently for their expressions to show disapproval. Those expressions showed love and excitement and Ellie felt the tension slowly fade from her tightened shoulders. Steven immediately expressed his love for Ellie and they both hoped the children would accept them as a couple. Everything was silent and Steven and Ellie both began to feel uncomfortable as they looked at each child and then at each other.

Suddenly, a shout from Annie reverberated. "One, two, three!" All in unison, the three children yelled, "Hallelujah, it's about time!"

As if held in time, Ellie and Steven just sat there, mouths agape, eyes set in a stare, and both were unable to speak. It seemed Annie, Abby, and Mark already knew, or suspected, that this dinner meeting was going to be about their parents. They must have been scheming for quite some time. Happiness exploded in the room and Ellie couldn't hold back her tears. They were all rising from their chairs and hugging Ellie and Steven and each other. Ellie noticed that Mark hugged Abby a bit longer than he normally would have, and she couldn't help but smile at the thought that not only had Mark been accepting of hers and Steven's relationship, but that he also had found a considerably deep fondness for Abby. This night just couldn't have been more perfect.

With all the goodbyes said, they left the restaurant. Ellie and Steven were the last ones to leave, and as they walked outside, Steven turned Ellie towards him and smiled his winning smile and said, "Ellie Barrett, I'm so much in love with you." He kissed her before she could respond, but as soon as their lips unlocked from each other, she immediately expressed her deep love for him also. They walked arm in arm across the street, streaks of dim light from the full moon splayed against her glowing face. They quickly got in the car and drove home.

The ride to Ellie's seemed to come to an end too quickly. She wanted to stay by his side forever – she didn't want this night to end. Never in a million years would she have thought that she could be this happy again. Years ago, Tyler had told her, "Ellie, never say never!" She silently whispered a prayer and said, "Thank you, my sweet, sweet Tyler."

All of the family seemed to be in agreement with this new relationship and because of this, every time they were all together their time became sweeter and more loving among all the children.

On this particular morning, Ellie bounced out of bed, donned her usual pink bathrobe, and walked into her kitchen. She glanced around the room and thought the area seemed brighter, more welcoming, and the entire aura of the house seemed to explode with warmth and excitement, but she couldn't quite figure out why she was feeling this way. Tiny giggles escaped her throat, and she began to hum one of her favorite "Oldies But Goodies" songs from her much younger days. She twirled and did a few dance steps, grabbed her pillow from the sofa and held it close to her heart as she smiled, laughed, and happily plopped her petite body in her favorite chair. Even the floral pattern on the chair seemed to come alive with a brightness she had never noticed before. Everything was beautiful and Ellie was about to explode with joy and happiness.

After having her second cup of coffee, she sauntered into her bedroom, still feeling elated. She wanted to call Steven and hear his voice, but decided to get her shower, get dressed, and then make the call. Before she could gather her thoughts and make her way to the bathroom, the phone rang. Hoping it was Steven, she quickly answered, and her heart melted. The soft, happy tone of his voice was exactly what she needed. Her day was already filled with excitement, even though she wasn't sure why it seemed to be so strong, but hearing his voice was the icing on the cake for her. They talked for several minutes and made plans to have lunch together at their favorite little cafe in town.

The air was crisp, and Ellie knew Fall would soon end and the birth of winter would arrive, bringing colder winds and a beautiful blanket of snow would engulf the little town. She always loved the winter, especially when she and Tyler would snuggle on the sofa and enjoy the roaring fire as it warmed them, the room, and made everything in the world seem right and peaceful.

This will be a new winter for Ellie and Steven – a time to reflect on their past several months of dating and sharing their thoughts and plans for their future. It almost seemed surreal. She never thought that she could be this happy again.

Lunch with Steven was wonderful, as usual. They laughed, talked, held hands, and stared into each other's eyes, making it almost impossible to have a conversation. It seemed that they each knew what the other was thinking. Every time they were together, their love for each other deepened, and bands of love wrapped tightly around their hearts. Ellie and Steven were in love, and nothing would change that for either of them.

<h1 style="text-align:center">*Fourteen*</h1>

Steven paced back and forth in his house, putting his hands in his pockets, then removing them. He continued doing this and felt giddy as he took his handkerchief and dabbed at the perspiration on his forehead. His hand reached deep into his pocket, and he felt the small velvet box. With shaking hands, he retrieved the box from his pocket and stared at it, finally lifting the lid slowly as he gazed at the beautiful pear-shaped diamond engagement ring. His mind began to race. *Will she like it? Will it fit? Is it too extravagant or possibly not extravagant enough? I'm hoping she is satisfied with yellow gold and not white gold.* Steven's emotions were running wild, and he knew that what he was about to do was something he never thought he'd experience again, not since his wife's death. He also knew that his love for Ellie was very real, and he couldn't even imagine his life without her in it. The time had come for him to propose to Ellie.

She answered the phone with excitement and heard Steven's soft voice. Every time he called her, she would practically melt. She felt like a new teenager who had just discovered puppy love, and she actually loved the feeling; however, she also knew this was no teenage love fling – this went much deeper and was much more mature.

They talked for almost an hour, not wanting to end the call. Finally, Steven asked her if she would like to go to dinner and that he would like to plan the evening for them. During the entire conversation, he was twirling the small velvet box in his hand, opening it and then closing it, repeating the process. They made their plans and Steven said, "Ellie, wear something special tonight. This isn't a ball cap and T-shirt night." They laughed because they had become so comfortable with each other that they often just wore jeans, T-shirts and ball caps for an informal and extremely casual night of hot dogs, burgers, and fries at the local Dairy Bar.

Ellie couldn't help but wonder why he wanted her to wear something special, but she immediately made her way to her closet and began the search. By the time she had finished sorting through her clothes, she realized she had a huge pile of everything from her closet now heaped on her bed. *Maybe I should call Annie and get some suggestions. No, I can surely decide on a dress for tonight all by myself.*

She stood in front of her mirror, holding up one dress, then another, then another. Black, red, emerald green, navy – and the color scheme went on and on. She placed them all back in her closet and tucked away in the end of the closet was a beautiful dress in coral color with a gold braid trim around the ends of the sleeves and neckline. She had forgotten all about that dress and wasn't sure it even still fit. She slid it over her petite body and as it inched its way over each curve, she was delighted – it fit like a glove. The hemline was just above the knees, showing off her tanned and shapely legs. The neckline wasn't too low, but it definitely needed the finishing touches of a necklace. The gold braid trim at the wrist of the sleeves fit tightly around her tiny wrist, accenting her tanned hands and well-manicured nails. She knew this was the dress for the evening with Steven. She even had matching shoes.

Ellie suddenly felt a twirling in her stomach, but just thought perhaps she was hungry since she had not eaten lunch. She felt fine but couldn't quite identify the problem or why she was feeling so antsy. She started to laugh as she thought about all the dates she and Steven had been on in the past several months and she remembered how her tummy always did a full work-out with excitement. This is exactly what this had to be - anticipation of their date tonight.

The doorbell rang and she elegantly walked to the door, heart pounding with excitement. Opening the door, she gazed at Steven. He was such a handsome man. He held roses in his hands, smiled his beautiful smile and said, "Ellie Barrett, I love you."

Her heart almost stopped at his declaration of love. Her smile radiated as he walked in, closed the door, and held her in his arms. He could smell her perfume and the peach scent of her shampoo. He knew he never wanted to let her go. Ellie felt the same way as she inhaled his cologne and the scent of his fresh shirt. They were so much in love. Their hearts pounded in rhythm as he held her close to his chest.

Deciding it was time to leave so they could make their dinner reservation in time, they walked to the car holding hands and letting their glances speak their unspeakable words.

The valet opened Ellie's car door and Steven was immediately at her side helping her out of the car. The restaurant was gorgeous – soft lighting and equally soft music. It reminded her of their first date at the elegant French restaurant. Her arm was wrapped around his and they entered, the wonderful aromas of food and all the waiters dressed in black and white with a white napkin draped across their arms. She knew this was going to be quite an evening and she was excited – and hungry!

They were seated near a fireplace, and she loved it. With the onset of winter, the small fire warmed her, and she could feel relaxation overtaking her body. She and Steven smiled often at each other, touched each other's hands, and at one point, he took her hand in his, brought it to his mouth, and kissed it. Ellie thought, *Just like in the movies!* She couldn't help but giggle, but she was thrilled at the gesture.

Their dinner was exquisite, and their waiter was very attentive, bringing them whatever they needed. She couldn't help but wonder if he was this attentive to all his customers; she was impressed. After dinner and dessert, the table was cleared, and Steven slid his chair closer to Ellie's and took both of her hands in his as he gazed into her eyes. She felt his hand trembling, or was that her own? *What on earth is he doing?* Her mind couldn't quite comprehend his sudden actions.

With his voice sounding a bit shaky, he began his rehearsed speech. He had stood in front of his mirror, holding the engagement ring, and had practiced his speech at least three hundred times. Now, suddenly, he was having difficulty finding the words.

"Ellie, I never thought any of this would happen. The first time I saw you working in your flower garden, then your trip to the house with your little basket for Abby and me, the huge "snake" I had to kill, and so many other things that made you so special – all of it has brought us to this moment. I am deeply in love with you, and I have no doubts that you feel the same way." He squirmed in his chair as Ellie stared at him, dumbfounded.

"Our children get along great and have been very accepting of our relationship and this makes us feel more at ease about our two families. I actually think they are hoping for more for us than just dating. Do you sense it, too?"

Ellie sat there, still dumbfounded, and nodded, but as she affirmed it, she also felt as if something was about to happen. Steven released one of her hands from his, reached into his pocket, and placed a black velvet box on the table, never taking his eyes off Ellie. His thoughts were bouncing around in his head. *This is it,*

Steven Monroe. The moment you've been waiting for. This is the proposal you have looked forward to. God has given you a perfect gift.

He opened the box and took Ellie's left hand. He removed the beautiful sparkling diamond, placed it on her ring finger and said, "Ellie Barrett, will you marry me and make me the happiest man on this earth? I love you with all my heart and I'm so thankful that God has brought you into my life."

Tears trickled down Ellie's face as she received the diamond ring, gazing at the sparkling facets as they reflected the lighting of the room and the candles. It had been many years since she had felt this way about a man – her first husband, Tyler. She knew in her heart that she was doing the right thing; that Tyler would approve of Steven and the happiness he had brought to her.

"Steven, I can't even begin to express how I feel about you and how I feel about this very moment. My heart is so full of love for you and to think about how God brought us together. I have no doubts that we will continue to be happy and explore the rest of our lives together. You are a treasure – you are MY treasure. I accept your proposal, and the ring is absolutely gorgeous. Thank you, my precious Steven. I love you!"

They exchanged glances, then kissed and sealed their engagement. Happiness oozed from them. They had been oblivious to anyone within ear range, but when the proposal was over and after the last "I love you," an eruption of applause and well wishes burst from other customers. Ellie blushed and Steven just grinned as they thanked the strangers for their well wishes.

On the ride home, Ellie kept stretching out her left hand and watched the brilliance of the ring as it shone as they passed streetlights, headlights, even the moonlight. It was like a fairy tale, and she was the princess rescued by the amazingly handsome prince. She couldn't help but giggle. They talked and laughed and squeezed each other's hands on the ride home.

She invited him in for coffee and they both knew they should be talking about the plans for their future, but first they had to tell their children about the engagement. Once again, they planned a meeting at a restaurant. She called Annie and asked her to call Mark and Abby. She tried to keep her excitement on a low keel as she explained to Annie that their last meal they all had together was such a fun night, that she and Steven would like to have another meal together. Annie promised she would tell them, and they would all be at the designated restaurant. So far, Annie didn't seem to suspect anything unusual.

Steven and Ellie talked for hours until they both began to yawn and agreed that it was time to call it a night. Ellie knew she wouldn't sleep at all; there was too much excitement brewing inside her. They made their plans to meet the next morning for breakfast at her house and would then begin to discuss wedding plans. Just saying those words made Ellie giggle with excitement. Steven loved her little gentle giggle, the way her nose wrinkled when she laughed. He just loved everything about her.

She walked him to the door, and they embraced for several minutes, kissing, and laughing, and holding each other. What a beautiful night to remember and she knew she would always treasure this night in her heart. They kissed once more and he left for his home, the sweetness of her lips lingering on his and a joy in his heart that he had not known for many years. God was so good.

When Steven left, Ellie began to do her little dance, twirling, jumping, swaying from side to side. She was too excited to go to bed even though she was drained from the evening's excitement. Rushing to her bedroom, she slipped out of her dress and searched for her pajamas – finally finding them under the mountain of clothes on her bed. Each time her hand moved towards the clothes, she would stop and admire the beautiful diamond that graced her hand. She wondered if he had selected this gorgeous rock all by himself or if Abby had helped. No, she knew Abby didn't know about this engagement. Steven would have told her if Abby had helped him decide on a ring. No, this was a moment in time that only she and Steven shared, but she knew in her heart that the children would be thrilled about the engagement.

Ellie looked at the heap of clothes piled on her bed, shoved them all to one side and slowly crawled between the sheets. As she turned off her bedside lamp, she took another glance at the sparkling reminder of her evening with the love of her life. She turned her hand in different directions, gazing at the ring's brilliance. Sliding her right hand gently under her face, admiring her ring on her left hand, she felt her eyes begin to close. Soon, sleep engulfed her body and she slept.

The sun shone through her windows and brightened her room. Ellie slowly opened her eyes and caught a glimpse of the beautiful diamond that still graced her left hand. This was not a dream; it was very real. Everything about the night before came rushing back to her mind and she smiled, giggled, and began to kick her feet and legs up and down on the mattress. She felt like the proverbial teenager in love, except this was not a passing fling as so many teenagers experience – this was real, it was deep, and it was forever; there was no doubt in her mind about this commitment.

A new day, a new life, and a new love; these were the things Ellie had hoped for and now God had brought it all to fruition. How could she ever thank Him enough for these blessings!

Fifteen

Ellie had no idea that getting engaged could bring on such excitement in her life. She was still young and had many years ahead of her if God allowed it. She also had reconciled the fact that Tyler would want her to be happy and have someone who would love her and take care of her. She also knew that Tyler was her first love and would always have a very special place in her heart. Today was the day that she and Steven would begin making their wedding plans.

The doorbell rang and like an eager teenager, she flew to the door and breathlessly flung it open. There he was! The gorgeous man she was so much in love with, stood before her with his arms open wide ready to embrace her with so much strength that she could hardly breathe. She loved it!

The table was set with coffee cups, plates, and her homemade strawberry streusel with warm vanilla glaze. It was also accompanied by a bowl of fresh berries and melons, cut to perfection. As Steven looked at the food, he wondered *Is there anything this woman CAN'T do? Everything about her is just perfect.*

They sat across from each other, still grinning and Ellie made it so obvious to use her left hand while serving so Steven could also catch a glimpse of her beautiful diamond. She was ecstatic. Carefully pouring the coffee and slicing the streusel, she placed it before him and then served her own plate. They held hands and Steven blessed the food before them, just as he always did before their meals.

Their breakfast completed and the dishes put away in the dishwasher, the time had come for them to sit beside each other and begin making plans for their wedding. There was so much to discuss – date, time, place, and then the plans for the honeymoon! It was a bit overwhelming for both of them, but exciting at the same time.

After several hours of talking and looking at amazing places online, they came to some conclusions. They set their wedding date for December 28 at 2 p.m. All the Christmas celebrations would be over and family members would have plenty of time to prepare to attend the wedding. She and Steven decided on a very small ceremony in the church. It would be mostly family and a few friends – nothing elaborate, just simple. A part of Ellie was hoping it would snow, but not enough to hinder anyone from attending – just enough to give it that special ambience, the scene that is portrayed on so many Christmas cards. All sorts of ideas were flying around in Ellie's mind, but all very exciting.

With the date and time decided, they excitedly talked about the honeymoon. Steven wanted it to be extremely special. They discussed the long list of possibilities but finally decided on a cruise to the Caribbean for 2 weeks. Ellie was about to squirm out of her chair as the plans were being made. She kept giggling and occasionally taking Steven's hand and squeezing it. She didn't know when she had been this excited over anything. They wanted everything to be decided before they told the children, and the decision was made that Ellie would take care of the wedding plans and Steven would make all the arrangements for the cruise. He would be there to help her in any way she needed him.

Ellie busied herself all day as she made preparations for the evening out with Steven and the three children. This was finally the night when they would tell Abby, Annie, and Mark that they were getting married, and it would give Ellie her grand opportunity to extend her left hand and show them her marvelous diamond engagement ring. She hoped they would all be happy and accepting of their news. In her heart, she believed they would be beyond excited for them. As she thought of the evening and how it would all play out, she felt so joyous and thankful that God had brought this family together. She intended to spend the rest of her life making sure they were a loving and caring family. She just didn't know how she could possibly be any happier. *Well, becoming Steven's wife will top it all,* thought Ellie.

He was right on time and greeted her with a gentle loving kiss. Ellie's mind went crazy. *I am going to love this when we are married; kisses every day and gentle loving by a man sent only by God to complete my life.* Ellie couldn't seem to quit smiling as she took Steven's hand and they left for the restaurant.

They sat in silence for a few minutes as cars whizzed by and streetlights seemed to bring out the brilliance of her engagement ring. There was excitement in the air and they both kept squeezing the other one's hand – sort of a silent message that whispered *I love you.*

Finally, Steven broke the silence and asked her, "Are you nervous?" Ellie shook her head and replied, "I'm not the least bit nervous, but I am filled with excitement. I know they will love this idea of us getting married and I can promise you that Annie will jump on the idea of going shopping for just the right dress for me." They both laughed as the lights of the restaurant came into view and they saw the three cars that represented the three children who were already there, probably with no idea what was about to happen.

Annie spotted them first and motioned for them to come to the table. Mark stood, hugged his mother, and shook Steven's hand. Abby and Annie gave their hugs to each of them, and everyone took their seats and began to chatter. Ellie purposely kept her left hand in her lap until just the right time to extend it for them to gasp at the beauty of the ring.

Dinner was delicious and the conversation most enjoyable and all over the place. Talk of work issues, Christmas decorating, new recipes – everyone chattering at once. Ellie felt so at ease with everything. She knew in her heart that this was going to be a wonderful family. Everyone seemed to enjoy each other's company and it all just felt so comfortable and so very right. Her heart raced with excitement. Coffee and dessert were served, and everyone was having such a wonderful time, sharing stories and happenings, and even plans.

Ellie squeezed Steven's hand under the table as a signal that now was a good time to begin to tell the real reason for the dinner gathering. He cleared his throat and placed his folded dinner napkin next to his dessert plate. They all sat back and took notice and knew something was going to follow, but they weren't exactly sure what it was. Abby knew her father well enough to know that he was about to say something rather profound. He always had a certain look on his face and his eyes would blink a little more quickly than usual. She prepared herself mentally and emotionally for whatever was about to happen.

"We've asked you all to meet us tonight for dinner for more than just as good friends. Ellie and I wanted you to all be here for a very important announcement." The three adult children stared at Ellie and Steven, mouths all drawn tightly, not knowing what was about to hit them. Ellie even sensed a bit of unknown fear in Annie and Mark. Abby looked away briefly and when she glanced back at her dad, Ellie saw a glisten of tears in her eyes. Were they tears of sadness or joy?

This was about to be the moment of truth. She prayed quickly and silently that the children would accept their news. Annie and Mark knew that Steven was very important to her and yet, she wondered if the memory of their dad was also creeping into their minds. *God, please take control of this situation and help them see that I can love again.* Ellie was used to making quick prayers in times of a quickly needed answer.

Ellie extended her left hand as Steven announced that they were getting married on December 28. She held her breath as the three children gazed at her ring, then at her, then at Steven, and back at the ring. She wasn't sure how long she was holding her breath until she heard, "WOW! That ring is beautiful." She wasn't even sure who said it, but suddenly the three were out of their seats and hugging and congratulating her and Steven. Annie was crying and Abby was looking for a tissue to wipe her own beautiful blue eyes. Mark, a little more reserved, hugged his mother and then hugged Steven as he said, "Welcome to our little family." By the time all the hugging concluded, everyone was either crying or showing signs of wanting to but holding back – that would be Mark and Steven. God had brought it all together and everyone was exceedingly happy. Then Annie piped up and said, "Mom, we just HAVE to go shopping for just the right dress!" Laughter filled the room as Ellie looked at Steven and said, "I told you so!" They embraced and he kissed her on the cheek.

The ride home was euphoric. Ellie and Steven were talking a mile a minute and re-living the night at the restaurant, so happy and pleased that their children were happy for them. Steven had planned to tell Ellie the plans he had made so far with the honeymoon cruise but decided to wait until they got to Ellie's house and could enjoy a cup of coffee, a roaring fire, and just the two of them quietly talking and planning. To Ellie, this night just couldn't get any better.

Doing just as they had planned, they sat in front of the fire and Steven began to tell her the plans. They would board their ship in Ft. Lauderdale on December 31, New Year's Eve after having spent the first three nights honeymooning on the way to Ft. Lauderdale. He had the cruise line's itinerary so Ellie would know exactly where they would be coming into ports. She had never been on a cruise and was excited beyond words. At this moment, they were bundled up in sofa blankets in front of a fire, but soon would be donning bathing suits and shorts. How exciting!

She suddenly became quiet, and Steven was concerned as he asked her, "Ellie, are you alright? Is anything wrong?" She started laughing as she said, "I really have to get with Annie and go shopping for some new island clothes with matching accessories!"

The embers in the fireplace continued to dim and the room was beginning to lose its warmth. Ellie had snuggled close to Steven and the two of them must have dozed. Her eyes slowly opened, and she gazed at Steven who was already lovingly looking at her while she napped. She stretched and wondered how she had been so blessed to be engaged to such a wonderful man. They both yawned as she apologized for falling asleep – total contentment. He seemed equally as content.

They kissed goodnight at the door and Steven left, feeling a bit saddened that he had to leave this beautiful woman who had stolen his heart so completely, but also knowing that in two months he would never have to leave her again.

The drive to his house, which was only a couple of blocks away, seemed a million miles from Ellie. He could hardly wait until they were married, and they would never have to be apart again. He began to pray and thank God for sending a wonderful woman into his life. He knew he would never be able to thank Him enough.

He had been blessed with a wonderful and loving wife for many years and together they had a daughter who had made them proud in so many ways. Their little family of three proudly claimed Christ as their personal Savior and they joyfully served the Lord in many capacities.

He recalled the day they received the news that his wife had stage four cancer and only had a short time to live. The treatments she took were no longer working and it was only a matter of a few months, possibly weeks, before she would go home to be with the Lord. Even now as he thought about it, his heart ached, but God quickly reminded him of the blessing that waited for him just a couple of blocks away and the joy and excitement returned. He would always have a special place in his heart for his first wife, but Ellie had already filled the surrounding area of his heart with her love for him. There was no doubt that this marriage was going to be exceptional. He would make sure Ellie always felt loved and appreciated. He would always be by her side for whatever she needed, and he would support her in anything she endeavored to do. He was truly a very blessed man!

Sixteen

Annie and Ellie had made plans to go shopping. Only two months and so much to do before the wedding! She had already reserved the church and Pastor Jim was excited to be officiating. The church would already be decorated with red Poinsettias and greenery and white candles. *I do have to remember to have them remove the manger and all the nativity props. Might not look too much like a wedding with sheep and shepherds.* Ellie couldn't help but giggle at the thought of hay scattered all over the altar where they would exchange their vows.

She and Annie shopped all day, and nothing really "jumped" off the dress racks that shouted "Wedding," so they continued to look in every store. She wasn't going to wear the traditional white or off-white wedding dress. This was going to be very simple and classy. She had already experienced the big wedding with the long dress and veil. She was young and wanted a fairytale wedding. She was much older now and all that frou-frou frills stuff no longer appealed to her. All she wanted was a simple suit and matching shoes. Actually, all she wanted was to hurry up and be married to Steven so they could begin their lives together.

Finally, with aching feet and an overwhelmed mind, they decided to try one more shop and then go home. They had both heard of Jen's Specialty Shop, specializing in cocktail dresses, wedding attire, and special event dresses and accessories. It was worth a try, so they entered. Ellie had never seen so much glitz and glamour and bling. She looked at Annie and they both laughed. She certainly didn't want to come down the aisle with flashing lights and sequins that glowed. They were about to leave the store when the clerk asked if she could help them. Ellie explained the wedding and what she would like to wear. The clerk, who was a bit older than Ellie, knew exactly what she was referring to and took her to another annex of the building. It was toned down to what Ellie was expecting – no glitter, glamour, bling or sequins, just simple dresses and suits. A renewed strength washed over Ellie as she began to look through the racks of clothing. And there it was! A simple cream- colored suit, classy, but not too overly done. There was a small bit of top stitching around the collar and the cuffs of the sleeves. Dainty pearl buttons graced the front of the fitted suit jacket that accented her tiny waist and perfectly shaped hips. The skirt was calf-length with a kick-pleat just high enough to give her movement when she walked. It was just what she had hoped for. The shoes were a soft cream-colored satin with small rosettes on the toe. Ellie was ecstatic and Annie just beamed when her mother tried it on. It was perfect in every way. They talked about how the outfit would look so beautiful against all the red Poinsettias in the church, adding to the glorious season they would have just celebrated. All Ellie needed to complete it would have been the angels singing as they must have done at the birth of Jesus on that Christmas season. Well, maybe she would just have to settle for the organ in the church. However, knowing Steven, he would have put in a special request for the angels if it had been the slightest possibility. He was such a dear, dear man and she loved him with all her heart. Being married to Steven Monroe was right at the top of her wish list for Christmas, and this was a definite wish that was coming true.

With the outfit complete, Annie and Ellie drove to the "Crazy Q" for some much-needed ice cream while they talked about the wedding and the honeymoon. The next item on their agenda was to shop for island clothes, but not today. That was for another day with rested feet.

Her cell phone was ringing as she was opening her front door. Carefully handling her gorgeous wedding outfit and shoebox, she rushed to the sofa, laid it all down and searched her purse for the phone. She already knew who it was but answered with anticipation. The soft gentle tone of his voice made her forget about her aching feet and tired back. She curled up on the sofa while Steven expressed his love for her and the big day that would be approaching soon, but not soon enough for him. They laughed, giggled, talked about her shopping day, and finally decided to go out to dinner later that evening.

Bubbles grew in abundance as she let the water run in her soaking tub. "Let's see," said Ellie, "I need bath salts, bubble bath, and coconut-scented moisturizing milk bath. Oh, my, I may never get out of this exotic bath."

She was laughing at the thought of slithering in this tub and filling the bathroom with such wonderful aromas that would probably permeate throughout the house. Steven was sure to know she had engulfed herself with a zillion different fragrances, but she also knew he would enjoy the softness of her skin. She had definitely moisturized!

With all the wedding and honeymoon plans completed, there were times that she felt as if the day would never arrive, and yet, there were days when Ellie realized that there were so many little final details to attend to. Each day and every tiny detail were engulfed with excitement and joy and anticipation. The days and weeks began to fly by as each day brought her closer to becoming Steven Monroe's wife. Just the thought brought little wiggly swirls of butterflies to her tummy.

Today for some strange reason, Ellie felt drawn to the picture and the framed American flag which graced her mantle. Slowly she walked toward the picture of her first love, Tyler Barrett, USMC. Her mind wandered, memories flashed, and her heart stilled for a moment. Gently, she held his picture in her hands and then to her heart as tears started to well up in her eyes. They weren't tears of sadness, but they weren't tears of joy either. She was confused and torn as she began to second-guess her involvement with Steven. Flying to the forefront of her mind came that statement she had made to Tyler so many years ago –*I will never love anyone else, and I will never marry again if anything should happen to you.* She then remembered Tyler's sweet voice and his smile as he said, *Ellie, never say never.*

She knew in her heart that Tyler would always be a part of her and would always be tucked away in a special place in her heart. Steven had never asked Ellie to remove Tyler's picture and he fully understood her hesitancy. He knew she loved Tyler for many years and together they had created a beautiful family. He would never be so selfish as to ask her to forget about Tyler.

Lovingly, Ellie gazed at the picture and silently thanked Tyler for all those years of love and patience and understanding; for giving her two beautiful and healthy children. The entire family stood on solid ground, spiritually, and Ellie knew that she would see Tyler again one day in heaven. She was so grateful for that strong foundation that she had loved and enjoyed for all those years.

Tearfully, she took his picture and the flag and carefully placed it in one of the guest rooms, which happened to be Mark's former bedroom. She knew as Tyler's son he would treasure it being in his room. Perhaps one day, she would give it to him or to Annie, but for now, it would remain in its place in Mark's room. This task was probably one of the most difficult she had ever had to do, other than face his death and the arrangements, etc. She wasn't "putting him away" so that he was no longer a part of her. She was just re-arranging her heart and making room for Steven. She had no doubt that Tyler would approve of Steven. She turned from the picture and slowly walked out of the room, leaving a small part of her heart resting next to her first love.

The calendar on the desk in the kitchen was finally turned to December. Skies were gray and the possibility of snow seemed to be the main focus on the weather channel on TV. Ellie knew there was still so much to do to prepare not only for Christmas, but also for the wedding. *What was I thinking, planning a wedding during the Christmas season? Everybody is already frantic with trying to get ready for the holidays and then I plunge ahead and announce a wedding three days after Christmas! Ellie Barrett, soon to be Ellie Monroe, you have lost your mind. Looks like everyone will just get gift cards this year.* She couldn't help but chuckle at the thought of friends and family opening an envelope and all that would be in there would be a gift card – no ribbons or bows – just a plastic gift card. Nope, she would do better than that. Christmas was always special in the Barrett household. Wrapping paper strewn everywhere, ribbons, bows, unwrapped gifts, gift receipts for those returns. And there was always hot spiced tea or coffee and lots of homemade Christmas cookies shared with bundles of laughter and sneak-peaks into boxes. Ellie wanted to make sure this Christmas tradition would continue, only this time, it would be with a different man and grown-up children. Nevertheless, it would be wonderful. She would make sure of that!

Glancing back at the calendar, Ellie knew what all had to be done and she also knew the time frame. The days were running into each other and if she allowed it, she would panic at the short time left before Christmas and her wedding day. Surely, folks would understand if every little decorating detail didn't quite measure up this year as in years past. Next year will be different. She'll pull out all the stops and decorate as if she was being asked to decorate the White House in Washington, D.C..

With the cold air hitting her in the face, she trudged on towards her car and kept glancing at the sky. Any minute, it would open, and a glorious display of beautiful snowflakes would surround her. She just hoped it wouldn't continue to snow so that everything stood still, and no one would be able to shop for gifts or food. She silently prayed for a beautiful snowfall, then a clearing, and all would be well for the wedding day. God heard her small prayer. After all her final shopping, she drove into her driveway, began to walk to her door and it happened. Softly and quietly, the snowflakes began to cover the ground and trees. Ellie stood at the bottom of her steps, looked up as little flakes touched the tips of her eyelashes and she smiled and simply said, "You're such a good, good God. Thank you."

Ellie and Steven sat comfortably on her sofa after enjoying a bowl of chili and a salad. Weeks ago, they had discussed living arrangements – her house or his, or purchase another home. It wasn't an easy decision to make for Ellie, but they had come to a decision that they would purchase another home and fill it with their own memories they would make together. Leaving her home where she had memories of Tyler and the children was going to be difficult to do, but she also knew that Steven deserved to be where he didn't feel he was living in the shadow of another man. They talked about living in his home, but then it would mean that every day they would have to drive by Ellie's house, and it could stir up old feelings and maybe even feelings of regret. Together they discussed every angle of it and both decided on a new home in another area of town. They had looked at lots of homes and had finally decided on one that was located on a beautiful lake. They had their own private boat dock and pier and they had already met their neighbors and found that they all shared so much in common. Ellie was eager to get to know them better and possibly find some new good friends.

What a blessing! The three children agreed to take care of all the packing of both homes and have everything boxed and moved into the new house by the time they returned from their honeymoon. With both homes already sold, Ellie felt the relief of not having to have those concerns weighing heavily on them as they honeymooned in the Caribbean. Just another one of God's blessings showered on them.

Where did it go? They had all enjoyed a time of family gathering for Christmas, opening presents, and having a wonderful time. The atmosphere was filled with love and laughter. Everyone was eager to help Ellie with the feast for this new soon-to-be extended family. Steven said the blessing, thanking God for this new family and for love and guidance for all of them as they begin to blend into one united family. Each person then added their own thanks. Ellie thought she would pop with love and thankfulness. This was everything she had ever hoped it would be. Love filled the room.

Everyone was stuffed and moaning and groaning about the over-indulgence and questioning their reason for doing that to themselves. But it was all said and done with a smile of total contentment on their faces. Ellie and Steven slipped away quietly and put on their coats, tip-toeing out the door to catch a glimpse of the gray sky and breathe the cold, but fresh air, little puffs of vapor escaping their mouths as they talked. They were both hoping for snow, but only just enough to give their wedding day the perfect picture postcard scene.

Returning to the warm house, Mark and Steven tended the fire and had it blazing and settled down to watch TV. Neither of them really cared about what was being shown; they both knew it wouldn't be long before their eyelids closed, and sleep would take over. Before they waddled to the den, they both offered to help clean up the dishes and kitchen. The girls all had it under control and really wanted to be alone so they could giggle and discuss wedding plans and the glorious honeymoon, which they did. Ellie, Annie, and Abby all moved with excitement as they were all talking at once and laughing. Ellie's heart was filled with love and joy for this wonderful Christmas celebration. Nothing could top the most important fact, that it was the birthday of Jesus, but just an added blessing with a family who would soon come together and gel as one. She felt that her heart would explode with love and happiness.

Only two more days and she would be Mrs. Steven Monroe. It just couldn't get any better! Everything was ready. Her bouquet would be picked up by Annie and she would meet them at the church. Mark would drive her to the church, and she would dress in one of the Sunday School rooms with Annie's help. Abby would make sure her dad was there and would help him in any way he needed, but mostly for moral support and to keep him from getting too antsy. He was more than excited about this special day. Pastor Jim would also be in the room with Steven to help keep him calm once Abby left to take her place for the wedding march. Mark would walk his mother down the aisle, present her to Steven, and then take his place beside Steven and serve as his best man. Steven had asked Mark if he would be comfortable enough to be his best man and Mark had happily agreed. Annie would be her mother's main attendant and Abby would be there as her other attendant. Usually, there is an usher for each attendant, but at this wedding Mark would usher Abby on one side and Annie on the other as the three of them would lock arms and proceed out of the church. This was the plan and Ellie prayed all would go as planned.

Rehearsal time! Everyone in the small wedding party met at the church and Pastor Jim was waiting for them. The church was beautiful and warm. A soft glow from the cross above the baptistery set the perfect atmosphere. Red Poinsettias were lined across the rostrum and down the steps of the altar. Interspersed among the bright red Poinsettias was an occasional white Poinsettia. The pews were all adorned with red and white Poinsettias in a triangular shape that almost touched the floor. Velvet bows topped each one. In one corner was a gorgeous Christmas tree filled with all the Christian symbols of Christmas and tiny lights. The sanctuary lights were dimmed which seemed to accentuate all the other decorations. Ellie knew it was going to be a wedding right out of a magazine. She was so pleased and so excited. In only 24 hours, she would be Mrs. Steven Monroe.

Pastor Jim went over the order of the service, and they all practiced their individual part. Satisfied that all was well, they all hugged the pastor and said goodnight.

With a sky that looked as if it would explode with snowflakes, they looked up, glanced at each other and probably had the same silent prayer. The five of them drove to the French restaurant where it all began – Steven and Ellie's first date. So much love and laughter filled the room for them as they dined on French delicacies. Steven and Ellie both expressed their love for the three children and their appreciation for their acceptance of this marriage. Ellie looked around at each one as they talked and laughed, and in her mind, she thanked God for this occasion and this new family. God had blessed them all and Ellie would never take any of this for granted but would always be thankful for this beautiful blessing.

It was agreed upon that they shouldn't be out late on this rehearsal night. A big day was waiting for them, and everyone needed rest. Ellie didn't know how in the world she would be able to rest or sleep – there was too much excitement in the air; however, the three children began to say their good-nights and go their separate ways. Ellie and Steven hurriedly walked to the car in the cold night air, ready to enjoy the warm heat from the car and hold hands all the way home. He walked Ellie to the door, went inside for a few minutes, long enough to hold her in his arms and kiss her gently. The looks exchanged between them spoke volumes. Tomorrow would be the day they had waited for. The day they would be joined as one and begin the next journey of their lives together. It was almost more than either of them could stand. With a reluctance to leave, Steven slowly walked to the door, his heart pounding and each beat quietly whispered, *I love you*. He kissed her again, and said, "The next time I see you, we will be joining ourselves as husband and wife forever. She held tight to him and smiled and said, "I love you tonight, tomorrow, and always, and I look forward to sharing my life with you." With those words resonating in his ears, he stepped out from the warmth of her arms onto the porch and made his way home – the last night he would spend in his house.

Alone in her home, Ellie walked from room to room, remembering events and recalling special memories that seemed to cling to the walls like tentacles that wouldn't let go. She only hoped the new owners would make their own special memories and would love the home as much as she and Tyler had loved it. Tyler! She walked into Mark's room where Tyler's picture and his framed flag were neatly placed on the nightstand. She had her own private conversation and felt a release from all the years of carrying so much hurt and pain since his death. It was as if Tyler was trying to let go so that she could now be free to love again and be loved by someone who would be everything she needed and hoped for. She slowly backed out of the room, gently turned off the light, and could still see the shadowy glow on the picture from the outside streetlight. "Good night, Tyler. I'll always love you. Thank you for allowing me to love again."

Seventeen

Ellie's eyes popped open, the red numbers on the clock read 9 a.m. "My wedding day!" yelled Ellie. The excitement and nervousness began to pump through her veins as she quickly hopped out of her warm bed. It suddenly hit her as she lightly tapped her forehead. "This is the last time I will sleep alone in this bed. Tonight, I'll share a bed with another man, my handsome and exciting husband!"

There was so much to do, but Ellie first had her coffee and her usual slice of banana bread. *Well, this probably isn't the most wholesome breakfast, but it's all I can handle right now. Someone has unlocked the caged-up butterflies and they're all in my stomach. I hope I can get through this with some sort of dignified decorum.* She laughed, giggled, jumped up and down like a kid, and ran to her bedroom to finish packing for their glorious Caribbean honeymoon. She laid claim to the entire world of happiness, excitement, love, and joy.

She watched the clock. There was no way at all that she could eat one bite of lunch. The time was approaching, and Mark would soon be there to drive her to the church. It was time to look at her "to-do" list and make certain that everything had been packed. It was all done, complete, and neatly organized. One last glimpse at the gold band that she had purchased for Steven. Inside the band the jeweler had engraved exactly what she had asked for. In a beautiful script font, it read *Our love is forever – December 28, 2022.* She wanted to engrave more but there was no more room. She would just have to tell him the rest of the message after they were married. Ellie couldn't stop smiling. She had a lifetime to express her deep love for him – and she would.

Watching the gray sky, Mark drove to his mother's house, ready to whisk her away to the church for this big event. When he arrived, he saw her peeking out the window and smiling. He knew she had been noticing the menacing gray clouds that hovered and threatened a change of weather, but nothing was going to ruin this day for anyone, especially for Ellie and Steven.

Annie ran out of the church to meet her mother and Mark. "She's all yours, now, Annie. The rest is up to you. See you in a little while." He hugged his mother, kissed her on the cheek and told her he loved her.

So much conversation, laughter, make-up, hair spray, and the final touch of lipstick. They could hear the lovely organ music drifting through the hallway. Abby came flying in the room, almost out of breath, she yelled, "He's ready!" Ellie's heart pounded even louder. She would soon be Mrs. Steven Monroe.

Mark appeared at the door and gazed at his mother, Annie, and then double-gazed at Abby. Ellie and Annie looked at each other and gave that *What's that all about?* look. Was a new love brewing?

He turned to his mother and expressed his love and appreciation for her and all her love through the years. "Mom, you look amazing. Steven is going to have to be resuscitated when he sees you!" The four of them laughed as they also tried to get control of their behavior. "Mom, it's time!" She picked up her beautiful bouquet of miniature red poinsettias interspersed with baby's breath and white satin ribbon streamers gently swaying on the stems of her flowers. She was gorgeous and she knew it.

"I never thought I'd ever be this happy again. Look at me – I feel so pretty." She thanked the three children for everything they had done and would be doing with the houses while they were on their honeymoon. Mark led a sweet, but brief, prayer for the occasion and for this new family of five. When he finished his prayer, all three ladies were trying to gently wipe their eyes without smearing their mascara. "Y'all are such girls!" said Mark while shaking his head, raising his eyebrows, and rolling his eyes. With that being said, they made their way to the sanctuary.

The church was full, which surprised Ellie. She knew she had lots of friends, but she had resigned herself to the fact that probably everyone would be home enjoying the holidays with family. Today was an outpouring and expression of their love for Ellie and Steven. She was thrilled.

The music began to swell, and everyone stood. Steven stood at the front of the church with Pastor Jim. They were both smiling. Abby walked down the aisle and took her place followed by Annie. The music stopped briefly and then *Canon in D.* by Pachelbel began to be played on the organ. That was the cue for Ellie and Mark to make their entrance. With her arm gracefully resting through Mark's arm, the two of them slowly walked to the altar.

Ellie and Steven couldn't take their eyes off each other as she came down the aisle and took her place. She just knew Steven and everyone else in the room could hear her heart pounding. Mark released her arm, kissed her on the cheek and whispered, "Mom, I love you. Be happy." He then presented her to Steven.

Her eyes were moist with tears, but they only made them sparkle against the dim lighting and candles. She handed her bouquet to

Annie and then took Steven's hand. It was trembling, but so was hers.

The ceremony was a brief one with each of them saying their vows to each other and exchanging rings. Pastor Jim read I Corinthians 13 – the love chapter that is so often read at weddings. Ellie had heard it all her life, but today it had a completely different meaning for her as she was joined in love and matrimony to Steven. It was all brought to light for her as never before.

After a prayer, Pastor Jim pronounced them husband and wife and told Steven to now kiss his bride. Ellie and Steven had never kissed in public and certainly not in front of their children, even though it would have been perfectly alright. They both could feel their faces turn a little pink with warmth as they embraced and kissed.

The music began and the little wedding party made its way to the Fellowship Hall. First the bride and groom, followed by Mark with Annie on one side and Abby on the other with their arms gently draped through Mark's and rested on his forearm. Abby snuggled a little closer and clinched Mark's arm a little more tightly than expected. He kept glancing at her as he drew her arm closer to his body. A slight blush began to creep up Mark's neck and face. Abby smiled and for the first time in a very long time, she felt completely content.

The Fellowship Hall was bustling with ladies carrying silver and crystal trays of food to the tables. Soft music was playing in the background and folks were lined up to speak to Ellie and Steven, hugging and wishing them much happiness. Ellie felt something pulling on the hem of her dress but just assumed it was someone whisking by and accidentally brushing against her dress. She dismissed it and continued to speak to the guests.

There it was again – the tugging on her dress. She turned and looked down only to see a little girl about three or four years old, dressed in a beautiful red velvet dress and white leggings with little Mary Jane shoes. The child kept looking up at Ellie and smiling. Ellie excused herself from the guests in line and bent to the little girl's level. "Hi. You are a very pretty little girl, and your dress is beautiful. What's your name?"

"My name is Hannah." Ellie took Hannah's tiny hands and wrapped hers around them, and said, "Hannah, may I give you a hug?" The child smiled and raised her little arms for Ellie to embrace. After the hug, Hannah whispered to Ellie, "You're pretty," and ran off to find her mother. Ellie was touched in her heart by the little girl's remark as she shared it with Steven. For the first time in a long time, she felt pretty; no, she felt beautiful – God's own personal touch to her inner being.

The evening was coming to an end and Ellie and Steven kept whispering to each other, while smiling and stealing kisses. It was time for them to leave the reception and begin their journey, not only to their honeymoon destination, but their journey for their lives together. Everything had been orchestrated by God and they both were filled with praise and thanksgiving for being brought together.

Saying their good-byes to everyone and hugging their children, they walked out of the Fellowship Hall and immediately stopped. Ellie looked up as the snow began to fall gently on them – the very thing she had hoped for was now taking place. Guests stood in the doorway and watched as Steven and Ellie kissed, waved one final good-bye, and made their way through a winter wonderland, snowflakes drifting and swirling, dancing like tiny ballerinas. It was a perfect night.

Already two glorious nights of their honeymoon had passed, and now they were in sunny Florida waiting until time to board the cruise ship. With total happiness and excitement, Ellie could hardly eat her breakfast. Two weeks on a cruise with Steven was more than she could have ever hoped for, but Steven made everything so special for her. She stared at her gold wedding band and the beautiful diamond ring that snuggly fit against it. Then she glanced at the gold band that encircled Steven's third finger of his left hand. It was perfect. They were perfect. This marriage was perfect. So many thoughts raced through her mind. Steven must have sensed that she was lost in thought as he reached for her hand and gave it a gentle squeeze and leaned towards her. "Mrs. Monroe, I am so much in love with you." They kissed one last time when they heard the loud sound of the ship's whistle echoing from the dock and letting them know it was time to board. Hand in hand they walked to the ship.

Once on board, and before the ship left the dock, Ellie stood at the rail and gazed at the beautiful blue skies and calm water, consumed with excitement. People of all ages were scurrying around trying to find a special place at the railing so they could wave farewell to their friends and family. She wondered if they could all be as happy as she was at that very moment.

Off to one side of the ship she saw a small cloud approaching. *Such a lovely shape, so white and so fluffy*, she thought, *but why only one small cloud in such a vast blue sky?* She watched as it drifted closer and closer to the ship. Ellie took Steven's hand in hers as the ship began to slowly leave the dock. She watched the cloud as it seemed to change shapes and become smaller. She squinted and noticed it gently beginning to dissipate. Ellie turned her head sideways and intently stared at the tiny remnants of the cloud.

She knew she heard it – a faint whisper streaming from that tiny puff of white. *Ellie, my love, be happy – and never say never!*

She almost spoke out loud. Was her mind playing tricks on her? *Did anyone else hear it? Did Steven hear what I heard?* Her heart was racing as she tried to hear it again, but there was silence, only the chatter of the people aboard the ship could be heard.

It was him! She knew it! It was Tyler releasing her and sending her his final message of love. She smiled and tightly put her arms around the man she would spend the rest of her life with. Tyler was right – *Never Say Never!*

A Note to
My Readers

Life isn't always what we hope for. Through the journey, we take many turns and detours – some are good, and some aren't. However, as we grow to maturity, we learn to cope and appreciate the blessings that God gives us every day.

God's Word tells us that in our lives we will have disappointments, heartache, and troubles, but He also tells us not to worry because He is greater than any of the adversities that we face. Christians are not exempt from all these calamities. We all know someone who has lost a child or a spouse, or a best friend. Possibly you have experienced one or more of these already in your own life. Perhaps you have felt that you could never find anyone to replace that special person in your life – maybe a husband or a wife who has been part of your life for many years. It just might be that God has already worked in that area and has given you someone to love and share your life with. If so, be thankful and praise Him for it.

It's very important to remember that God's Word tells us that in the midst of heartache and disappointments that hit us all from time to time, He is faithful to His promises when He tells us that He will never leave us or forsake us. Just knowing someone will always be there for us brings relief. People of this world will fail us and cause us hurt and pain, but God will not. Personally, I have found Him to be constantly listening to my prayers, my cries, and even my anger. The reason He does this is because He understands. We must remember that He also went through some horrible endurances, too, so because of what He experienced as a man gives Him full understanding of what we face in life. We must also remember that not only was He Jesus, the man, but He is also God.

I love praying to my heavenly Father. My prayers aren't those of great orators, but just simple and from the heart. It's easy to pray for my husband, my children, and grandchildren, and my extended family and friends, but I know God also wants to hear my requests for my life, too. I believe He loves it when I go to Him for the things I personally need, and when I ask Him to help me become the woman He wants me to be – the woman He needs me to be to others who are in need of kindness and love.

One of my favorite places to be is on my porch early in the morning or when the sun is going down and the night sounds of all the little critters can be heard. It's a perfect time to spend time alone with God, thanking Him for putting me on his list of "wake-up calls" each morning. Every day is precious and even though I don't know what lies ahead for me, I am still grateful for being allowed to be part of it. Will I make mistakes during the day? Of course, I will. We all do. Will He be there to correct me through the Holy Spirit's nudge? Always!

Some of my friends think I'm a bit strange because I love feeding the little squirrels that live in all the trees surrounding our house. My husband and I buy bagged corn every week and each morning I spread it all around to feed God's little creatures. I love watching them as they scurry around, sitting up with their little white tummies bulging. They have a special old tree stump they like to sit on and hurriedly nibble on each kernel of corn. It sort of reminds me of people. We are constantly in a hurry to get what we need, we have to finish a task, to meet the demands of our family or our bosses. We finish one task and rush to find another one that has a deadline. Forever rushing! We hardly find time in the day to stop and spend a few moments alone with God. That's when we get into trouble – we feel we must meet everyone's needs and we put God on a back burner someplace and forget about Him all during the day. We fill our minds with mundane things and scurry around, just like the little squirrels, hurriedly switching from one task to another and then another. We exhaust ourselves.

As I watched the squirrels, I noticed that some of them were burying their corn kernels and peanuts, preparing for the winter. They have no way of knowing that I will be feeding them all during the winter, so they make preparations. Others were gobbling up the corn as quickly as they could, hurrying before another squirrel could take it away from them. Oh, my goodness, I couldn't help but, again, think of people – always hurrying to get what we can, needing (or just wanting) something more, something better and bigger than our friends have, working, working, working! Let me ask you a question. Is God in all of this? Have you considered what He might want for your life? He always provides exactly what we need. From time to time, He even gives us added blessings and things we didn't ask for, but He just wants to give them because He loves us. He's a good, good God. Believe Him and trust Him for all your needs. He never sleeps and He's always ready to hear from you.

When I wake up in the middle of the night for no apparent reason (sometimes that's my own personal thinking), I take that time to pray. It's quiet and I believe He woke me up because He wanted to hear from me, and He wanted to talk to me. Maybe I was being too busy during the day to find time to have a conversation with Him, so He would wake me in the middle of the night so I could give Him uninterrupted time. I always begin by thanking

Him for my salvation and then I move on to other blessings He's given to me. Names of different people will pop into my head, and I know it's Him urging me to pray for them, which I do. It's a privilege to pray for people and I don't take this privilege for granted. I love talking to my heavenly Father. Sometimes I spend time praising Him and other times I spend time asking for mercy for those friends or family who are going through a difficult time.

Never underestimate God's miraculous workings in your life. Never fail to share those times with others. Be a witness to His grace and mercy in your walk with Him.

When you begin to doubt if He will answer your prayers, stop, and remember what He did for you when He died for your sins and gave you a hope for a future with Him. He will answer in His own time – a time that is best for you. Don't doubt, and remember, *"Never Say Never."*

Judy

About the Author

Judy Giddens Sheriff is a retired educator with a Ph.D. in Christian Counseling who does extensive counseling with people going through separation and divorce. Judy teaches divorce recovery workshops and is available for group seminars on the subject. She enjoys speaking at women's conferences and has been the keynote speaker on numerous occasions. She is also an accomplished musician and has served as church organist, pianist, and choir director. She received degrees from Mars Hill University, Greenwich University, and Newburgh Theological Seminary. Judy and her husband, Richard, both natives of North Carolina, enjoy singing as a ministry outreach. She has two children and four grandchildren.